Dear God,

I hope this lands in the right hands and we can make magic

HOT LII

WRITTEN BY:

EL'DRICA HUDSON

Copyright © 2020 El'Drica Hudson

Published by El'Drica Hudson

Pittsburgh, Pennsylvania

Cover design by Shawn T. Blanchard and Team @ University
of Moguls Publishing & Design

Library of Congress Cataloging-in-Publication Data

Hudson, El'Drica, 1992-

For more information for sales and/or to order book please email:

eldrica.hudson44@gmail.com

www.Whoopistclair.com

Follow El'Drica Hudson on all social media platforms

@EldricaHudson @whoopi_stclair

TABLE OF CONTENTS:

I.   DEDICATION / 8

II.   ACKNOWLEDGEMENT / 9

III.   A LETTER FROM MY MOM / 11

1. PREFACE / 12

2. INTRODUCTION / 13

3. A VILLAGE FULL OF SAINTS / 15

4. BREAKING NEWS / 26

5. ORIGINAL CUTT GIRLS / 49

6. WAR / 66

7. ENEMIES / 73

8. THE SUPERHERO / 79

9. NUMB / 87

10. PROMOTION TO THE GAME / 94

11. SUMMER VACATION / 115

12. ENOUGH IS ENOUGH / 148

DEDICATION

This book is dedicated to my son Daryl and daughter Amier. Writing this book took a lot of time and effort away from you two. Mommy is securing our future. I'm showing you both what hard work and dedication looks like. I'm paving the way for us. Thank you both for being patient and loving me unconditionally.

This book is also dedicated to my mother Deanna and sister El'Micia. I love both of you unconditionally. My first family before I created my own. Being my moms oldest and my sister's "big sis" made me responsible, independent, brave, and powerful.

Finally, I would also like to dedicate this book to my neighborhood, St. Clair Village. I can never forget where I come from!

ACKNOWLEDGEMENTS

I would like to acknowledge all my family and friends for the unconditional love and support. You all constantly reminded me of how bright my light shines.

To the family and friends of those who lost their life due to gun violence, police brutality, and drugs. Stay strong!

To those on welfare, growing up in a bad neighborhood, and the innocent that are locked away in prison. Continue to fight! Never give up!

To everyone from my neighborhood that taught me something valuable. It takes a village to raise a child and you all did an amazing job with me.

Finally, I would like to acknowledge my higher power, the creator, for using me as a vessel to spread love and positivity across the world.

With peace, love, and positive energy.

Thank you!

A LETTER FROM MY MOM

My daughter, El'Drica Hudson, born January 31, 1992, has always been a loving child. Since she was a baby, people always gravitated to her. She didn't learn how to walk until she was two years of age. Not because she couldn't but because everybody always picked her up and carried her in their arms. I remember when I first gave birth to her in Mercy Hospital, I knew she was going to be special. She immediately brought joy into my world. I could feel it in my heart. She made my heart smile soon as she opened her eyes.

From that day forward, she's been very intelligent, well-mannered, and resilient, with a beautiful soul. Every waking day, she makes me feel like a proud mom. She's a go getter/hard worker just like me. El'Drica, on all occasions, has a great sense of humor with a huge heart and a bright and beautiful smile that can weather any storm.

30 years later, and she still thriving. She made me a first-time mother back in 1992 and gave me my first two grandchildren, who I adore, tremendously.

Her journey continues and I'm glad to be a part of it. My baby is so talented, who knows what she will do next.

God sent me an angel. El'Drica is heaven sent.

~Deanna Hill

PREFACE

Thank you for picking up this book. Its more than just a hood novel. In these pages are deeply personal stories from the trenches, where I spent eighteen years of my life. It's an insight on what it's like to grow up in the projects as a young woman. Usually when there's a light shined on woman it's about SEX. Us, woman are underestimated in life. SEX doesn't define us. We are powerful human beings. I enhanced into a dominant woman because of my environment. I grew into an entrepreneur because of my environment. I gained an understanding on how to be skeptical, but learn to listen, growing up in St. Clair Village.

I wrote this book to get it off my chest, sort of speak, and it was very therapeutic. In any circumstances, not once, was I ever open to speaking with a therapist. That was considered snitching in my neighborhood, so this is my outlet. I am releasing my past and creating a better future. Henceforth, I'm turning my trauma into trophy's.

I hope this book save many lives. I pray it bring someone out of that dark space and into the light. I was alone writing this book but alone for greatness. To prosper and to tell my best version.

INTRODUCTION

They say in life there are only two types of people, leaders and followers.

I disagree, I strongly feel that people overcompensate to try not to fit one of those labels and the others to try to fit the other.

I believe there are two types of individuals, but not leaders and followers, selfish and selfless people.

Selfless people should be what we strive to be in life.

Instead, we all develop a crab in the barrel mentality somewhere in our life.

When we learn to shed that mentality and embrace the selfless mentality the world will be better off.

So, as you embark on your journey through Summers life try not to embrace the selfish lessons she had to learn but focus on the selfless times that helped to shape Summer into a woman. Selfless individuals prosper while selfish people get ahead only to be pulled down by another selfish person.

Embrace selflessness!

~Wisdom from Kevin Watson

CHAPTER 1- A VILLAGE FULL OF SAINTS

"To survive, the people in neighborhoods are going to have to secede"

-Karl Heiss (American speechwriter)

The day started out just like any other, well not really, I guess you could say it was atypical. It was Wednesday and a school day but not for me, because I was at the beginning of the end of a 10-day suspension. For any kid that would surely spell strict punishment, but hey, I'm 13 years and 44 days old and 'smelling myself' as the older women would say. As I stepped out onto the porch trying not to be noticed, the smell of dampened mud and marijuana filled my nostrils. I looked around to find the source of this pungent smell at 9:30 am. It was like that in the hood, 9 am and it looked like midday, people out and about, older guys huddled up shooting dice for money and smoking weed. As I looked toward the street to view the newly purchased Lexus ls400 my mom popped up in yesterday, I noticed someone leaning on her car and then I heard my mother's voice "did you even brush your teeth before you opened my door?" So much for going unnoticed, but I wasn't about to let that deter me. I started out towards the 'cut'—short for shortcut, the cut was a long walkway that ran through half of my neighborhood and connected each court on one side and ran on the outer edge of a wooded area.

Before I move any further, allow me to introduce myself, my name is Summer. A lot of the older people, who never remember my name, call me little Bo in honor of my mother. The neighborhood we live in is St. Clair Village, a housing project on the South Side of Pittsburgh. It's a housing project isolated from the rest of the city that sits on a steep mountain top. Made up of 4 streets. Fisher Street, which is the first street entering St. Clair Village. Cresswell Street which connects to Fisher Street midway through the housing project. Bonifay street, which runs off Cresswell Street and runs right back around onto Cresswell—a big circle, then there's Kohne street which basically divides the neighborhood.

I was born and raised on Fisher Street. Being that it was the first street, we nicknamed it Up top.

On Cresswell Street we had a Recreation Center, a Playground, basketball court and an outdoor swimming pool. Just before you entered the neighborhood was a candy store. It wasn't much but we made the most out of it.

Ok now that your familiar with where this book takes place let's continue…..

I made my way to the cut before my mom could halt my momentum, and then made my way towards the neighborhood store 'little village' to get my day started off right with the usual bag of sunflower seeds, a Flintstone candy sugar straw and hot sausage. Walking to the store was an adventure in itself and at any point in the day could prove to be prosperous. Since little village sat down on Kohne St. I had to make my way down the cut and pass a bunch of older folks who usually asked me to buy them something from the store and then allowed me to keep the change for my troubles. Doing this, I developed my own little hustle which in the grand scheme was exactly 'little' when compared to what goes on in the neighborhood.

St. Clair Village had all types of illegal small businesses being ran in and around the neighborhood. A few small indoor candy stores, Miss Shirley had fifty cent Icey cups, Mr. Jukebox sold beer, shots of liquor and singles—which was cigarettes sold one by one or better put, stick by stick. We had a lot of weed sellers of course, but Reebok and his twin brother Red had the best weed. I called their house the GAS CHAMBER. We had a door you could knock on for blunts and plenty of doors you could knock on for any drug of your choice. The ice cream Man, Narley, would ride the ice cream truck through the neighborhood twice a day. Auntie Pickle & Uncle Dice ran a gambling spot. They had card games with multiple tables, dealing tunk, spades, lottery, pokeno, and bingo. Miss Valerie and her kids had basement parties with a two-dollar admission fee. We had a house that sold dinners. You could knock on Ms. Bo's door, my mom, and get your hair done, best believe she is going hook you up. My mom did straight back braids, plats, twisties, dreads, and any other style you could think of. She wasn't a boutique type of woman who styled ladies' hair with weave tracks and glue, her main customers were the men. You could catch a chick selling stolen clothes out the trunk of her car. Cousin Greg rode around in his yellow pickup truck with the grill installed and sold the 'bombest' pieces of grilled meat. He always had a sample for me, but it came at a price. I used to run up to his truck and put my cold hands on the side and yell "Cousin Greg, can I get a sample?" he'd come from the other side with his grumpy voice like "Not until you tell me who Madam CJ Walker is and how she made history!" I love Cousin Greg because he always put me to the test. Soon as I go quiet and start thinking, he would jump back in the truck and start up his engine like he's about to pull off "Wait, I know her, I just forgot what she did. Hold up! Let me think! She was a black entrepreneur?" Cousin Greg would turn the truck back off and his eyes would light up. "You on to something young lady" and then I'll know I had my sample now. "Continue" he'll shoot back. "Uhm, she sold something and became the First Black Self-made female millionaire."

"So, what did she sell?" He always had this grin on his face as he starts cutting me a piece of grilled chicken dipped in his special spicy BBQ sauce. "I don't know Cousin Greg, I forgot" He would hand me my sample and then I knew I had his attention and knowledge for the next 20 minutes, which usually came with more samples and more stories. I love to learn so I'm usually all ears.

He always began his history lesson in his old man voice "See, back in the late 1800 to early 1900's, slavery ended and us Niccas was just getting over the hump. Madam CJ Walker moved to Pittsburgh from Detroit in 1908 for just about two years. Her hair product business was booming, and Pittsburgh transportation system was fast and easy for her. Pittsburgh also known as Steel City come from good ole steel and she needed our services for her hot combs."

He was a Vietnam Veteran, and he was very wise. He looked good for his age. He was my grandma's nephew. He had many stripes on his belt and he always told me I was intelligent and that I would be a great woman when I grew up. All I had to do was be the best me and make it out of this Neighborhood. I believed him too.

He and many other people were fond of me. I never knew why but I was always grateful for the folks in my life. They were great to me. St. Clair was written for me.

"Maktub" As I learned later in life from a novel by Paulo Coelho titled The Alchemist.

The name St. Clair village can be misleading because it was far from a village of saints, but I'm one of the few lucky saint-like souls to make it out of a very dangerous place. There was an ongoing neighborhood feud with a neighborhood named Alpine Park, also on the south side of Pittsburgh. This feud raged for many years and took a lot of good lives, but that's for another time as right now the only thing on my mind is getting my fix. As I made my way towards the store, I was hoping to run into my uncle which was almost a sure thing since his 'trap house' which he nicknamed 'headquarters' was one court away from little village. The prospect of seeing my uncle always quickened my step, knowing I could surely get another dollar. I didn't really need it but hey, I'm a hustler and the goal are to get more money than you spend. That just how it was in the hood. We all were on the grind all the time.

The government didn't provide any real legal businesses, so we created our own. We had to survive in the projects.

St. Clair Village was a public housing project of the Pittsburgh Housing Authority. Originally built in September 1953, it housed over 1,000 African Americans families. It fell into disrepair and financial difficulty and was completely demolished in September 2010. Unfortunately, there were no businesses built in my community. It consisted only of residential houses and that's where we fell short learning how to survive without any legal job opportunities within the community. Some sold drugs, others went to the malls to steal and resell clothes, some picked up a gun, while others fell to the drugs that were being sold.

My mom used to do hair, hustle, and gamble, while my dad was one of the biggest drug dealers in the city of Pittsburgh. He was the guy who pulled up in his brand-new Mercedes Benz with spinners on its rims, a toothpick hanging from his mouth and had a mink fur coat on in the middle of winter. He and my mom were never really a great couple in my eyes. In my younger days all I really remembered was my mom always yelling and screaming at him, and him standing there looking guilty and dumb. He was a real drug dealer. Fancy cars. Nice clothes. Big jewelry but uneducated. So, he had massive females using him for his money. He was currently messing with some lady two doors up from us. That's when my respect for him completely disappeared. I spent a lot of night staring at the pictures on my walls, tossing and turning while my mom blasted Mary J Blidge all night long cleaning and waiting on my dad to come home. School nights was the worst. 2:22am I always caught that time on my digital clock. An hour later, I would hear him come in. I would hear the door slam, the music cut off, and then the arguments begin. Sometimes they would fight, and sometimes I would hear the door slam again. Then the music would come back on. I began to dislike my dad because of how he treated my mom and how he made her feel, which before long, began to appear on her really well. She would smoke cigarette after cigarette, singing the saddest of the saddest Mary J Blidge songs. Her all-time favorite, "Not Gon Cry" was always on repeat. I didn't understand how or why Mary used to say she's not going cry and my mom would be crying. Shit, honestly, I used to be in my room crying as well. I prayed a lot for my mom to leave him so it could just be me, her and my little sister. She didn't need him. We didn't need him. He wasn't a father figure to us. He didn't do anything fatherly around the house. He never helped us with homework or spent time with us. He was an outside dad. A holiday dad. Holidays was the only time I remember my mom happy. My mom knew how to hustle too so she didn't need his drug money. My mom's hustle was more secretive than my dad's "in your face" hustle. She had every pair of shoes you could name but she wasn't as flashy as my dad. Her hustle seemed calmer and less flaunted too. I don't know why she stayed with him for so long. At a very young age I knew that wasn't the love I wanted. He wasn't a real man in my eyes. He had all this money but my mom and his mom, my grandma lived in the projects, and that never sat well with me.

But anyways, it wasn't the worst of the worse and far from the best of the best, but it was my life. St. Clair Village was my neighborhood and I loved it. It made me who I am today. I repped it with my blood, sweat and tears. I used to scream it proudly "DARCCIDE!" That's what we called it! Born and raised for 18 years straight—the last 18 years that St. Clair stood tall.

What I learned more than anything living in St. Clair Village was how to LIVE ONE DAY AT A TIME. Everything happens for a reason and to never give up. My neighborhood shaped me to rise above.

IT CAN START IN THE PROJECTS BUT IT DON'T HAVE TO END THERE!

CHAPTER 2- BREAKING NEWS

John 3:16

"For God so loved the world, that he gave his only begotten son, that whosever believed in him should not perish, but have everlasting life."

MARCH 16, 2005

Today was about to change my life forever.....

"Breaking News! Reporting live with chopper radar. A High School student shot and killed as he sat outside his school. The high school was put on lock down immediately after the shooting left one dead on the scene and two seriously wounded. This investigation is unfolding right now. No names have been released. Police say the victims just walked out of this school behind me and was gunned down in the flash of a moment. We will be keeping you updated with more details as this tragic incident unwinds."

A man interrupts "Can you tell us whether the victims were students and if any suspects were taken into police custody?"

News reporter comes back on. "Again, all I can tell you Thomas is, a homicide detective stated that one died on the scene, all the victims were males who just left this high school. So far, no arrest has been announced but we do have homicide detectives on the scene and choppers in the sky. We will have live updates from Allegheny County police headquarter all throughout the morning. Thank you! I'm Veronica Sasukic from channel 12 news, back to you Thomas,"

"Yes, thanks Veronica we have family members of students arriving on the scene. No one is permitted in or out of the school. Again, the high school is on lockdown. Stay tuned for live coverage coming up at 11am."

"Now here is your daily weather from Joseph Galen."

With the map of Pittsburgh showing clear skies on the screen monitor, Joseph Galen appears. "Good morning America today is Wednesday March 16, 2005, and the time is 10:04 am. The sky is clear as we predicted, and the temperature right now is 67 degrees Fahrenheit which is very comfortable for commuters coming in and out of downtown Pittsburgh. Slight chance of rain showers is in the forecast later this evening, but right now it's a beautiful Wednesday morning."

As I walked back inside my house from the store, little village, and headed straight upstairs, I heard my mom change the channel from the news and grab the house phone to make a call. I was swift up the stairs, skipping two steps at a time, trying to avoid her because my eyes were red, and I was feeling a buzz from the blunt I just hit coming back up the cut. If she knew I was smoking she sure would have whooped my ass. I was only 13, but you couldn't tell me nothing.

As I entered my bedroom, I felt a weird energy form around me, it was almost as a ghost flew past my body, but I was high, so I shook it off. I closed my eyes and flopped backwards onto my queen-sized bed, my Grama just gifted me for my thirteenth birthday.

Lying flat on the bed I opened my eyes and starred at my ceiling wall. My celebrity crush Bow wow was starring right back at me with his straight white teeth and hazel eyes. I put him there so he could easily be the last person I see when I went to bed and the first person I see when I woke up. I had many other rappers and singers all over my bedroom walls, but Little Bow wow was the only one on the ceiling. I love music and Lil Bow wow was popping. He just came out with his #1 single "Let Me Hold You" featuring former B2K member Omarion the Friday that just past, mind you, it's only Wednesday and I already had every word in my head. "Down down around Atlanta Lanta Profound aye body know now, what I'm trying to do. I say Down Down Around Atlanta Lanta

Profound I'm trying to get chu to Let me hold you down, Down Down around Atlanta Lanta Profound" LOL "That's my shit" was my thoughts as I bobbed my head smiling hard from ear to ear.

Lol, I knew I was high as I kept giggling and rapping goofy like out loud "Down Down around, banana nana momond." Lol only hitting the blunt about 3 or 4 times I knew based on how giggly I was acting exactly where that weed came from "THE GAS CHAMBER MAN" (In my scary voice).

Lil Bow wow eyes on the poster started staring at me too hard and I saw tears form in his eyes as I stared back.

Seconds later,

I jumped up and went into the bathroom to wash my face like Craig did on the movie Friday, but that didn't work. So, I sat down on the edge of the tub resting my chin on the inside of my hand.

Thinking about all my friends in school, I had nothing to do until they got back to the hood. I had all morning to relax and patiently wait for our school bus to drop them off. Out of nowhere, I got chills, so I decided to run me a hot steamy bubble bath. I tip-toped downstairs quietly to steal some dish washing liquid from the kitchen to put in my bath water. Quick way to make bubbles when you from the hood. I poured some in the palm of my left hand while my right hand supported the dripping liquid coming through my fingers and ran back up the stairs on my tippy toes hoping my mom didn't notice me or the dish washing liquid I just stole. She would have a fit. I could hear her now. "Did you pay for that? I didn't think so! Since you like bubbles, when you done washing up, COME DOWNSTAIRS and WASH THEM DISHES IN MY SINK! ALL OF EM!" I was already on thin ice, and I hated washing dishes, so I was extra cautious around the crib. Of course, she wasn't paying me no attention because she had her ears to the phone as she laid on the living room couch, but I was high, so I was very paranoid. After about the 12th step I stubbed my big toe and wanted to scream, but I then hopped the rest of the way back into the bathroom carefully, not wanting to spill the liquid that was already dripping through my fingers and onto the floor.

"Whew this water feels bomb" was my only thought as I relaxed in the hot bath water. One thing about St. Clair Village is we had some hot ass water and on top of that, it was free. St. Clair was the projects, the hood—low-income housing. The residents, including my mom, only paid rent, everything else was included and her rent was based off her income. We lived good in the hood. We had cable, plenty of food from food stamps we received from Welfare, my mom had a nice car, and we had gear. Me and my little sister were two years apart. We were like oil and water, we didn't mix. I was the older child— Same daddy but different fathers. That will be explained later, right now this hot bath water and that blunt I hit prior to walking into the crib was the vibes. I just closed my eyes and removed every thought out of my head.

As soon as I got comfortable, water nearly touching the top of my neck, I heard a painful scream.

"iiiiiiiiiiiiiiiiiiiiiiiiiiiiiiiiiiii"

It wasn't coming from downstairs, it seemed to be coming through the bathroom window. I kept calm. But the voice was very familiar so I tried to listen for more screams to see if I could pick up on it.

PAUSE

"Noooooo, this can't be true! Nooooo! Homies Noooooooo! Them Motherfuckers killed my brother at school."

I recognized that voice and every word spoken. I jumped out the tub, grabbed my towel, and dashed to my room so I can quickly get dressed to go outside and see who, what, and where this tragic news was coming from. In the hood you didn't ask no questions, you could feel when something was wrong.

Mind you my house was the third house from Da Cut, so soon as I hit the corner the drama hit me smack dead in my face.

My vision got blurry, but my ears were wide open. Everybody in the next court was crying and yelling and holding on to one another like something unbalanced just happened. People get killed every day in the hood, but this feeling was different. This one hit home........

Home is where the heart is.......

Witnessing Tim break down in tears as Karesha tried to console him only brought tears to my eyes. I felt numb because I knew exactly who his brother was. What I wasn't apprehending was him saying that they killed him at school. Who would kill somebody at school? Only white kids did that, was my thoughts. As I got closer to get more information someone tapped me on my shoulder. When I turned around it was Crackhead Seedy asking me what happened.

Shrugging my shoulders, I replied "someone got shot at school, I think it was Tim's little brother."

"Naht uhh, who Little Leo? Didn't he just come home?" Crackhead Seedy asked.

I just walked away because deep down inside I couldn't handle what was taking place.

Feeling lightheaded I began thinking about how I lost my virginity to my secret crush last month. He told me not to tell nobody because he was three years older than me, and he was in high school. I was only in the 8th grade and had just turned into a teenager. My secret crush missed my 13th birthday, which was on January 31st, because he was locked away in a juvenile institution for troubled boys. He was released February 10th, after doing 6 months. He had a release party at his God mom's house where he lived because he lost his parents in a car accident a few years back. His Godmom was the best! Her name was Nicole, and she was so nice, she let him do anything. I often wondered if she allowed him to get away with so much because he lost his parents at a young age and she felt sorry for him, but I never spoke a word about it because his parents were an emotional topic. Miss Nicole used to let him have company, and they could smoke weed inside the house. He always had parties. He stayed fly and had all the Jordan's and throwback jerseys with the hat and headband to match. He even had two dirt bikes and a quad. She used to smoke with him and have conversations about a lot of things my mom wouldn't dare discuss with me. That's why I liked her—because she was down to earth. I always gave her respect because that's how I was raised, and she knew me and him had a thing for each other. She even encouraged it, often mentioning how cute and chocolate I was and how pretty my mom always kept my hair.

The night he was released from the juvenile institution he had a party, and during his party he told me to go upstairs in his attic and wait for him to come up there. It was getting late and the party in the basement was still jumping off the walls, which meant it was going to be a long night. I politely excused myself from my friends in a sneaky way, telling them I had to go to the bathroom, but I think they knew what I was up to because Leo was giving me the eye all afternoon and I didn't make it no better because I was blushing the whole night. When I made it upstairs, I was so nervous because I knew what was in store for me. We wrote each other the entire six months. We planned to have sex the exact day he came home, which was supposed to be my birthday, but his release date got pushed back due to his Godmom missing the appointment with the phone company for his house arrest monitor. The day had finally come, and I became a new woman. I was walking and talking funny. Nobody could tell me nothing. I was getting in trouble a lot more in school and my grades were dropping from my attendance. 3.2 was my average GPA but as I mentioned earlier, I was currently suspended from school for fighting on the school bus.

(Snapped out of thought)

Back to reality

I ran back home feeling queasy like I had to vomit. Everything around me seemed to be moving in a slow circle. When I busted through the front door my mom was walking out at the same time. Suddenly caught off guard, I passed out right in her arms.

What seemed like moments later, I awoke with a cold compress on my forehead and jumped up from what felt like out of my body. I was puzzled and wondered what I was doing on the couch. One of the neighbors was standing over me looking like she was dissecting a frog and I started panicking while she began calming me down. I see my mom walking back from the kitchen with a rag in one hand and a lit cigarette in her other hand. She started going off, "What the fuck is wrong with you Summer? Scaring me half to death. You know you passed out right? Were you smoking? Were you coming from Da Cut? Did you hear about Little Leo?"

With that last question I came back to my senses. I felt a sharp pain in my heart and in the bottom of my stomach. I tried to get up but was still a little lightheaded and flopped back down.

Fanning the cigarette smoke with my hand, I spoke out "Mom what did they say about him? Turn the news on. I got to call his Godmom"

My mind was racing, and I was looking around for my Cricket Phone but then realized my mom took it because I was suspended. "Mom can I have my phone back, I need it!" "Omg Is that it" pointing to the tv "Turn it up."

What I was witnessing in front of me was petrifying

There were dozens of police everywhere, students in bunches crying, then I seen what I didn't want to see. His brand new 2000 Audi Convertible that his Godmom just brought him not even two weeks ago.

"16-year-old shot in car at Olivertown High School" was in BOLD letters.

The news reporter starts to speak, "A ninth-grade student at Olivertown high school was killed this morning in a drive-by shooting a few hundred feet outside the school, just a month after someone tried and failed to kill him outside his Olivertown home.

Two other Olivertown students with him were wounded, one critically.

Leo, 16 was sitting in the driver seat of his blue Audi convertible parked behind Olivertown High on Southwest Street when a gray Honda Accord containing at least two men stopped beside it, according to police.

At least eight shots were fired into the vehicle. Police believe the driver of the Audi Convertible was absolutely the target.

Leo was shot once in the head and once in the torso. He was pronounced dead at 9:58 a.m., according to the Allegheny County coroner's office. His friends, whom names were not released was shot in the arm, in critical condition, while the other was only grazed by broken glass.

"Turn it off" was all I could murmur. I began sobbing in my hands because the love of my life just got murdered and I didn't know how I was going to carry on my life without him. He just took my virginity. We were in love. We had big dreams of getting married on my Prom night, which was 4 years from now, but now it was all ruined. He was gone forever. I kept our little secret between us and now I was lost. I can't believe he got killed outside of his school.

My mom must have known I was hurting bad in the inside because when she turned the TV off, she handed me my phone and walked away to the front porch to join the regular crowd that usually gathered, which today seemed more crowded than ever before. Grown-ups gossiping and being nebby. Weed and more cigarettes burning because of the current incident that just took place.

I looked down to my phone and noticed I had seven missed calls and two unread messages. I immediately ignored the call that was coming in to go to my unread messages, and there he was 6:30 am sharp texting, "Good morning Beautiful! I luv u!"

Then I noticed another message from him at 7:45 am stating "I got a surprise for u after school," Shaking my head I started crying hysterically and then my phone started vibrating again.

"Yo?"

"Best friend you hear about Leo and them?"

I couldn't respond.

"Yo Summer?" "You cool?"

"Where you at?" Was all I could utter.

"Bout to get off the bus by ya house, come outside." Hangs up.

That was my best friend Veeta, she must have left school early because it wasn't time for our school to close for the day. I got up slowly and walked outside to meet her at the bus stop, trying to ignore the old heads who tried to make conversation with me. I hugged a few of them because they demanded it, asking me if I was alright but I didn't want to talk to nobody but Veeta. I had to tell her about me and Leo. She the only person that would understand me and how I was feeling right now.

NOON!

"Homies Bytch I can't believe you didn't tell me all of this before" Veeta said loudly as she rolled up a blunt. We were upstairs in the bathroom of one of the abandoned houses where we usually skipped school to go and smoke.

I was crying silently, and my face had started feeling numb from all the tears. I couldn't wait to hit the blunt so it could take some of my pain away.

"I know Vee, what am I going to do?"

"I don't know but what I do know is, you got to stay strong, they definitely seen who did it. Slim was in the back seat and Eli was in the passenger, Homies I know they seen somebody pull up beside them."

"Homies they had to. The news said one of them was in critically."

"I think Eli got shot in his shoulder and Slim got grazed by the window shattering."

"Karesha talked to Slim before they took him to homicide, he told her he thinks it was Black and his right-hand man Stacey."

"Say Homies!"

"HOMIES!" Veeta reassured me.

"Bitch as Black? On everything I love I will kill his girlfriend, his sister, and his mom about my baby, HOMIES." I said balling my fist up.

"You got a lighter?" Veeta asked.

I shook my head No as I was wiping my face with my T-shirt, trying to pull myself together.

"Fuck! Let me call Kim, she was trying get an early dismissal too. That hoe always got a lighter." Veeta said pulling out her Boost Nextel phone.

"Homies, but never got no weed." I replied jokingly.

We chuckled a little but deep down inside nothing was funny. I just lost my man.

We heard the front door of the abandoned house open and got shook. Being nosey I hushed Veeta and flipped her phone down to hang up from calling Kim so we could be quiet.

"Nicca wzup? You riding or not Cuz?" I recognized that voice easily. That was definitely "Do Die" He didn't give a fuck about nothing. Hardcore young nicca. Rumors around the hood is he just left a nicca stinking by the neighborhood store for stealing his snap. In the hood all the hustlers had their own drug addicts whom they sold drug to, and they called them "snaps." Do Die wasn't really a hustler, he was more of a shooter. He got his name because that's exactly what he's about. "Do or Die."

"Man Bro, Homies Little Leo been disrespecting niccas since he came home lowkey. I don't know I got to think about it."

"Fuck u talmbout? Think about it? Nicca our click nicca just got smoked outside his school and you talking about u got to think about it?

U know what, homies you right! Think about it!"

(BOW) the sounds of one single gunshot went off.

"Bitch ass nicca" was all we heard, followed by dead silence and then the door slamming.

Frightened and terrified as fuck, me and Veeta knew we was at the wrong place at the wrong time. She signaled to me with her eyes that we needed to get out of here, but I was afraid to be seen leaving out the front door. I was frozen. She started nudging me to go but my feet wouldn't move. She creeped out the bathroom and down the steps. I followed as slowly as possible. Once at the bottom, on the 3rd and 4th step down, I noticed blood splattered on the wall. I grabbed Veeta's hood of her hoodie and took baby steps past who appeared to be Big Boy Roy. But with his face halfway blown off I wasn't sure. Soon as we got outside, we took off running. We ran in no particular direction but ended up at the dumpster right beside the St. Clair Pool.

Out of breath and scared as fuck we looked at each other as if we were trying to be sure through eye contact if we just heard and seen the same damn thing take place. I seen a tear roll down her face as I began to vomit everywhere.

What a fucking day and it was only Noon!

Two souls taken by Noon.......

By 12 o'clock in the middle of the day.....

The highest point......

I've told the kids in the ghettos that violence won't solve their problems, but then they asked me, and rightly so "Why does the government use massive doses of violence to bring about the change it wants in the world?" After this I knew I could no longer speak against the violence in the ghettos without also speaking against the violence of my government"—Martin Luther King Jr. (American minister, activist, & leader of the civil rights movement).

CHAPTER 3- ORIGINAL CUTT GIRLS

"We are only as strong as we are united, as weak as we are divided"

-JK Rowling (British writer, author of Harry Potter).

(Ice cream truck music playing)

Me and Veeta sat at the park waiting on Kim. We vowed to not speak a word to anyone about Do Die or Big Boy Roy. We knew better. Hear no evil! See no evil! Speak no evil! Them was the codes of the street. We were the Cutt Girls! It was me (Summer), Veeta, Kimba aka Little Kim, April, Ciara aka C C, Kayla, and Karesha.

Before I was introduced to the world, resting in the womb, I had entrepreneurship. I was born a hustler. My mom and her best friend made a bet on me when she was nine months pregnant with me. My arrival date was January 28, 1992. On that very same day my mom's best friend made a bet for $100 that I wasn't coming until February. They taped the hundred-dollar bill on my mom's stomach and right then and there my skills were developed. 12 hours before February, on January 31, I was pushed out into this world and my mom won the bet. I wasn't born with a silver spoon, but I came out winning.

I grew into a tomboy from living in a court with all boys. We played kickball, basketball, football, you name it. I was Dark-skin, boney and knock-kneed with thick long hair and perfect white teeth. The boys in my court used to tease me for being the blackest and they called me "Whoopi" Referring to the Actor Whoopi Goldberg who I knew from 'The Little Rascal,' 'The Color Purple' and 'Sister Act'. The name kind of stuck to me because I liked being the blackest and I love Whoopi's movies. I couldn't wait to grow up, get dreads and act.

I started hanging with the Cutt Girls in 6th grade. We had to stick together in Middle school because we shared it with our rival neighborhood, Alpine Village. Elementary school was all St. Clair village kids, but Middle school was different and farther from the neighborhood. I seen a fight jump off at recess during a Double-Dutch game and the rest was history. St. Clair kids came out on top and from then on, we were big and bad. Sitting together at lunch and hanging after school was the new norm. I was tired of hanging with the guys anyway. We were growing up. My breast was getting bigger, and I was having menstrual periods once a month. It started becoming complicated wearing a huge pad playing football, plus the guys always wanted me to play center so they could get their free feels. The worst was having cramps while I'm the next batter up in baseball. Kickball was bad too. Imagine being bloated and getting hit with a bouncy ball in your stomach. I don't mean to sound dramatic, but it was time to put a skirt on and paint my fingernails pink for once, plus Leo was getting sexier and sexier and my body was enjoying his eyes and soft touches every time we made contact.

Veeta was the strongest of the crew. Nothing scared her. I never seen her cry until today and that was just one tear. She was the go-to friend. She had all the good advice. Me and Veeta was total opposites. If she said No, I said Yes. I was loud and funny; she was quiet and mostly observed. I was the skinny friend while she was the fat friend. She was lighter than me, I would say she was brown skin. She had gear and money too that's why I like hanging with her, plus she had all the good snacks. Her father was one of the biggest drug dealers in the hood and that's how she got the name Vee-money. She was just as spoiled as all the spoiled kids up St. Clair Village, but she knew how to save. She was the oldest of six children, so she was very independent and responsible. We clicked almost immediately when we started hanging in school. She was the start of the fight that took place in 6th grade. Vee was turning the ropes on the double Dutch and some Alpine kids came running past, and one of them tripped causing some chocolate milk to spill on Vee. I didn't see all that. I just remember a lot of commotion and fist being thrown. She was normally very quiet and only spoke when spoken to.

Kim was the fighter of the crew. She always wanted to fight. She was the ratchetest of us all. She was the reason I was suspended in school and banned from the school bus. She didn't give a fuck about nothing. She was "Darccide" for life. The hardest, cripping, dancing, fighting hood princess. She was the short friend but had the heart of a Pitbull. Always on the go. She was the youngest of four sisters. Dark skin, pretty puff ball wearing, deep dimples, and petite. We called her the "Pitbull in a skirt." My mom didn't like me hanging with her, she said she was the reason I was skipping school, smoking, and cutting up. Kim's mom worked daylight shift, so she was either at work or at her boyfriend's house.

She basically gave her crib to her four daughters so yeah, we skipped school a lot at her crib. My mom was right about that part, but I was providing the weed so she couldn't blame Kim on the over end.

April was the cousin friend. She was all our cousin someway somehow. She wasn't around as much because her dad moved her and her siblings out of the hood. She came around in the summer and sometimes on the weekend. She was the sneaky, shy friend. Her dad thought she was so innocent. She was a daddy's girl. But she was the one fucking before all of us. We called her AP because she loved them Alpine Park boys and it was short for her real name, April. She was the turn-up friend. When AP was in the hood, we were always going to a party to have a good time. She had the best vibes out of all of us. We needed her around from time to time, and we really needed her energy around right now. Her energy was always good. She had the prettiest hair out of all of us. She looks like the little dark skin girl on the "Just for me" perm box. Her dad signed her up for a lot of beauty pageantry. She won a few when she was younger but when they looked at her address, things changed. Her dad immediately moved them out the hood but being a beauty pageants wasn't really April's dream. It was her mom's dream. Her mom passed away from Breast Cancer when April was only ten months old, and her dad stepped up and did all he could for her and her older siblings. He was a great dad. Better than mine in my eyes but what you see on the outside isn't always what's going on inside.

Ciara and Kayla are twin sisters. They grew up rough. Their mom was a crackhead, and their dad was a drunk. They had to steal to support each other. Rumor has it that their mom used to sell them for crack. Kayla was a little slow. They said it was the birth defects from their mom smoking crack during her pregnancy. We all protected Kayla like she was our own sister. Ciara, a.k.a. CC, was grown for her age. A little stuck up wearing high heels and booty shorts every day. They say she act like their mom the most. Always chasing boys. We all felt bad for the Twins. We would pitch in and buy them food and give our old clothes and shoes to them. They were less fortunate but had potential to outgrow their circumstances. Everybody always looked out for them.

Karesha was an only child. Her and Leo's older brother Tim was boyfriend and girlfriend. He lived with her and her mom. They had a son together who just turned two years old. They were a lot older than us. We were all 13 or 14, Karesha and Tim was both 19. She's the one who taught us all about sex. I will never forget our weekend sex lessons on them late summer nights. She was always on us about shaving our underarms and pussy hair. She taught us so many different sex moves, and my favorite was how to ride the dick and how to play with his pubic hairs while you moved up and down making sure not to fall off. She was nasty and open, and we needed someone like her around because she was the motherly one out of all of us. Who else to learn some sex advice from but Karesha? She was the first one out of all of us to have a baby so in our eyes she was an expert. She grew up in the court that was connected to the City Steps, so she knew everything because that's where everything went down.

We were the "Cutt girls" we all were raised up in different courts. But the Cutt was the connection that we all shared. We grew up in the Cutt. We would meet up in the Cutt. We fought in the Cutt. Smoked our first blunt in the Cutt. We laughed in the Cutt. Rumor has it, last summer, April lost her virginity in the Cutt.

Although we were young teenagers, we were used to killings and drive-bys. Firecrackers and gunshots sounded the same. Seeing crackhead leaning over in the middle of the street was normal. Just as normal as seeing older ladies getting their ass beat by their man. With that being said, what me and Vee just heard in that abandoned house that we had no business being in was normal. We learned to shake things off and keep it pushing. I'm not saying it's the right thing to do, but the odds were better that way.

We heard the ice cream truck from a distance, and I knew I still had credit from my uncles tab. Veeta's dad had a tab for her too so we both was prepared and knew what we were getting. We stopped Narley the Ice Cream man, got our goodies off the truck and decided to walk up to the Cutt.

We recognized our hood niccas sitting on the city steps. The City Steps was a landmark. It divided Da cutt in half. The city steps consisted of about sixty-six steps. It was a mountain to climb walking up but running down was fun. If I missed my bus in the morning at my bus stop, I would hit Da Cutt, run down the city steps, then boom my bus would be coming around the corner. We rode our bikes down the city steps sometimes too, however at a major risk. The city steps were like the spine of the hood. And looking at them now our spine was broke, and we were paralyzed. Everybody looked crushed. I felt that unbalanced feeling again. I noticed so many young black hurt faces. Everybody was sad. Everybody was looking for answers. Leo was the heart of St. Clair Village. He had this energy in him that made you incline towards him. At least that's what I felt every time our energies intertwined. He was a handsome chocolate younger version of the rapper Jadakiss to me. He talked funny considering he had a LYST. He had that Daffy Duck voice, and every time he would mock me, I would laugh so hard. I miss my baby already. I couldn't believe I wouldn't be hearing his funny voice again.

I pulled my phone out and dialed his number 444-0852 and his voicemail picked up immediately. I pushed the phone closer to my ear just to listen to his voice.

Bone Thugs N Harmony's song was in his background "Thuggish Ruggish Bone" "Heltho? Heltho? (In his Daffy

Duck voice) Who this? Hahaha sike nah you reached a Thuggish Ruggish Bone's Voicemail. Do your thing afther the tone." (BEEP) I started hysterically crying again. At this point in time, my face was burning from all the salty tears streaming from my eyes.

I observed the old heads gathered on the city steps and spotted my uncle and Veeta's dad at the bottom discussing something that seemed important. From Veeta's dad's hand gestures and my uncle's vital face expression, I knew something was about to go down either tonight or first thing in the morning. I couldn't take no more deaths. My heart was beating triple times already particularly after witnessing what just happened thirty minutes ago.

When my uncle and Veeta's dad noticed us, they immediately stopped talking and hugged us both. I'm an uncle's girl so I melted in his arms and started hysterically crying. He felt my pain and hugged me tighter, reassuring that whoever did this was going to feel our pain. I believed him too. I knew what was in order....

Retaliation was mandatory....

"We all about to hop in the ride and head to Leo's God mom's house. Y'all coming?" Veeta's dad asked.

"We still waiting on Kim, did y'all see her?" she replied.

Her dad yelled up the city steps "YO, ain't Little Kim up there?"

The first person who answered was Do Die.

"Yea old head she right here"

Chills went through my body hearing his voice, my uncle noticed. "You cool Neicey?" Hugging me again. "You are going be alright, uncle going handle this." I just started crying again.

Walking up the city steps, Veeta's dad instructed on who was riding with who and told us to get in the car with Lady Gee so we could stop at the store, grab some food, liquor, and bags of ice. Lady Gee was cool, she ran errands for the old heads. They trusted her, most of all, they trusted us with her.

"DoDie, you and Tone riding with me and Goat, bring them things too" Veeta's dad demanded. Lifting his shirt up and doing the Crip walk. DoDie responded "Old head what's my Motherfucking name?" Showing his chromed-out Glock.

A few of the fella's giggle. I can admit DoDie had a sense of humor, I was just always scared of him. My uncle dabbed him up and we all began walking to the curb to jump in the cars that was lined up along the street.

Leo's house wasn't far from the hood; however, it was near the enemy's territory so all the hood niccas was extra cautious.

"Damn Summer, you ok girl? You look bad?"

"She's not in the mood Kim," Veeta answered for me.

"We all lost somebody today Vee, she ain't special" Kim snapped back at Veeta, although the comment was intended for my reaction.

"Listen Kimba, not today. I got a headache and my stomach hurt from that ice cream," I lied.

"Well since your stomach hurt and you captain save a hoe, I'm sitting in the front seat," Kim said referring to the both of us.

"I don't give a fuck girl, who cares about the front seat?" I said rolling my eyes.

Sometimes Kim can be very competitive. She had it rough growing up with older sisters. She always thought everything was a challenge. She was also very big headed. We had a love hate relationship. When it was just us around each other she was very open to me and we talked about a lot of deep issues, but when she had a crowd, she loved to perform.

As the guys loaded up in their cars, we waited for Lady Gee to unlock the doors. She ran back to her house to go get something. Running back out, she rushed to the car and unlocked the doors.

Me and Veeta stood at the back doors while Kim claimed the front.

"Let Summer get in the front Little Kim." Lady Gee said as she motioned to the car.

Kim sucked her teeth and I smiled at her showing my pearly whites. She shoved me as we switched positions and I just let out a giggle. She was livid.

"She always gets to ride in the front," she said like a five-year-old child.

Lady Gee didn't respond to her nonsense. What she says, goes.

We jumped in the car and soon as she started the engine, Usher Confession part two blasted through the speakers. We rolled down our windows and rode off in the wind.

"My Boo" by Usher and Alicia Keys came on right after. We all started singing out loud. "There's always that one person who will always have your heart, you never see it coming because your blinded from the start. Know that you're the one for me it's clear that everyone can see, oohh babyyyy" We all had our arms in the air snapping our fingers doing our dance. "OH, I don't know about y'all but y'all know about us."

We all sang together.

We were feeling it.

"Lady Gee can we smoke in the ride?" I turned to her and asked. "As long as I hit it first!" She replied. I immediately smiled and turned my body towards the back seat extending my hand out. "Yo Kim give me a light!"

She pulled it out her blue jean baby phat purse and twisted her lips up. "Say Please!" Vee snatched it out her hand and handed it to me. Vee knew the vibes, and that's why I fucked with her the most. She always had my back. Kim didn't know the state of mind I was in, and I knew if she knew she would have had a nicer approach but she's a fucking Scorpio, so I ignored her. I lit the blunt, put it in Lady Gee's mouth and turned the music up to its capacity. We were smoking and vibing. Weed relax your mind and Music is for the soul. At that very moment, my mind and soul needed it.

Once we approached Olivertown we stopped at the gas station for ice. Then we stopped at McDonald's to grab us a quick bite after that nice blunt. We all had the munchies.

CHAPTER 4- WAR

"Those who are at war with others are not at peace with themselves."

-William Hazlitt (English essayist)

"Is that Shay Shay?" Kim yelled out.

Me on alert "Homies that's her."

"Slipping!" Vee added.

She was standing outside the McDonald's with some dude who appeared way older than her.

"That bitch snucked me when security broke up the fight on the bus," Kim remembered.

Veeta was already out the car and Kim and I was one step behind her.

"Yo Shay Shay wzup now? Homies I want the fair one," Kim demanded.

Suddenly caught off guard Shay Shay started backing up to go back inside the McDonald's.

"Hold up, hold up! Yal not about to jump her," the dude spoke out.

"Naw we not" I reassured knowing damn well when Kim was finished with her, I was getting several hits in.

"I don't want to fight you Kim," she uttered but Veeta was already on her ass like white on rice.

Grabbing her hair and swinging her to the ground instantly. Veeta threw two blows and blood started spraying out of Shay Shay's nose. She had no fight in her.

Me and Kim started stomping her at the same time, releasing all our frustrations. The dude tried to grab Veeta, her grip was too strong, so he pushed past me and Kim to pull Shay Shay off the ground. Once that didn't work, McDonald's employees began running out to break up the fight.

We heard Lady Gee yell out. "Let's go yal I'm riding dirty." Riding dirty in the hood usually means two or more things. One, the state inspection stickers are expired, two, you're driving without a driver's license, or worse, you have some sort of illegal drug in the vehicle. We all stopped with satisfaction in our bodies. We all ran to the car and jumped back in, peeling off faster than a race car. Our adrenaline was pumping. Kim and Veeta was in the back seat cracking up and I just leaned my seat back and started thinking about what just took place. Then Juvenile song "Nolia Clap" came on. We got rowdier as we zoomed the rest of the way to Leo's house.

Soon as we turned on his street, Lady Gee turned the music down for the respect of the neighbors and my stomach began turning in knots.

We parked and jumped out to join the crowd that was already gathered. So many people were outside Leo's, it was unbelievable. I didn't know this many people cared about him.

"Yo these little bitchs is off the chain" Lady Gee giggled and said to one of the old heads as we approached the crowd.

"They just jumped out on some poor little girl and dogged walk her literally."

"Say Homies!" "What happened?" A few of them asked.

I wasn't interested in telling the story, I continued to make my way through the crowd hugging familiar faces as I searched for Leo's Godmom.

As I proceeded toward the doorway, I recognized Leo's Godmom Nicole sitting in the rocking chair crying in the hallway. I went in and gave her a hug. I instantly started crying with her. She never looked up. She just hugged me back putting all her weight on me. I knew she was crushed. "I'm sorry Godmom" I finally managed to utter. She noticed my voice and finally lifted her head. "Oh, Summer baby they took him away from me." She spoke.

"I know I know; I can't believe it. You're the first person I thought of soon as I heard," I responded. She got up and took me to his room. Once inside, she locked the door for privacy. I flopped on his bed and got a whiff of his smell. My heart was in my stomach at this point. She walked to his dresser to get something. When she turned around, she handed me a belt buckle with my name on it. It was bling out with diamonds. She handed it to me and started telling me how he wanted to get me a late birthday present for my birthday but couldn't think of nothing I liked. "He was going to give you this today. He was crazy about you girl, had me at the mall for hours the other day," she said with a sad smile on her face. "I know, I loved him Godmom. Who would do this to him?" I said holding back tears trying to stay strong for her.

"We don't know yet, but that damn school have surveillance cameras all around so they going to tell me something."

"He wasn't perfect, and he made a lot of bad choices, but he was my baby. I promised his mom and dad I would protect him. I failed all three of them," she spoke with such pain as she flopped on his bed beside me.

"You did the best you could for him. He loved you so much. He was growing up. You couldn't control nothing that he was doing," I had to let her know this was not her fault. "You were all he had after his parents died. He wanted to give you the world when we grew up. That's all he talked about."

"Now he's gone forever, so young. I had to identify him at the morgue," was her last comment before someone knocked on the bedroom door and interrupted us.

(Knock knock) "Hey Nicole? Channel 12 news is out here, they want to talk to you."

His Godmom got up exhausted and prepared herself to go outside to talk. She wanted answers so she knew she had to get on TV and plead to the public for information.

"You coming?" She turned around and asked.

"No, I'm going stay right here and take a nap" I replied starring down at my new bling out name belt. I couldn't believe Leo never got the chance to give it to me. I felt his presence just by being inside his bedroom.

"Ok Baby girl I'll be out front," she said as she walked out of the room.

I climbed up on Leo's bed gripping his favorite pillow. It was a blue bandana pillowcase with a Tempur-Pedic pillow inside. It smelled exactly how I remembered him. Tears gathered in my eyes. I removed my red and white Air Force ones, shut my eyes and drifted off into my sleep hoping when I woke back up it would all be a dream.

CHAPTER 5- ENEMIES

"You have heard that it was said, "love your neighbor and hate your enemy." -Matthew 5:43

St. Clair Village had enemies of course. We had a major ongoing beef with a neighborhood named Alpine Park also known as AP.

Darccide and AP used to get along very well until the crack cocaine era came about in the early 1980s. Darccide hustlers started going to Alpine Park to hustle and the AP hustler didn't like that. So, they demanded their territory and then the war began, the rest is history. Now here we are in the middle of a beef we were born into. Only thing that separated the two neighborhoods was a white only neighborhood name Olivertown. I called it the white only town because up their people weren't running from threats, they were running for exercise or walking their expensive dogs. We only had Pit bulls in the hood. Olivertown had poodles and Yorkies and well-trained dogs on leashes. Olivertown was much larger than St. Clair and Alpine put together.

That's where the legal businesses were being ran. Grocery stores, Beer distributors, Banks, restaurants and many other businesses were at an all-time high in Olivertown. My Middle school was at the beginning of Olivertown, and Leo's High School was at the end of Olivertown. There was a fire station and two libraries in Olivertown. They even had their own police department called the Olivertown Police Department.

The police were real assholes and dickheads to everyone in my neighborhood.

So, there you have it. The Southside of Pittsburgh, PA consisted of two all black neighborhoods and a majority of white people neighborhood in the middle where all the businesses were located. We had to enter Olivertown for our household supplies and other things like school and work. The other options were to travel twenty-five minutes away to another location if you had a vehicle. We had public transportation, however the buses only ran every hour and a half and stopped running after 8pm. The bus route was around the circle of St. Clair, thru Olivertown, and then Downtown and back.

The two rival gangs would meet in the middle, but nothing would occur because there were surveillance cameras everywhere. Police was everywhere in Olivertown. Eventually the shooters figured out other ways to shoot up places and not get caught so that's how drive-byes started. Doing a drive by was going into the enemies' territory with a stolen car and shooting up the place. This way was the only way for the shooters to not get caught. They would go back to their neighborhood, ditch the stolen vehicle and bury the dirty guns.

This beef happened way before my time, but here we are in 2005 and I'm pretty sure Leo was murdered by someone from Alpine Park. I heard it was Black and his gang and that's probably who DoDie, Tone, Veeta's dad and my uncle was about to go search for.

Black and Leo had beef for years. They fought every time they seen each other up Olivertown. Soon as Leo was released, his God mom's home was shot up and rumor was that he retaliated the next day and was in school telling people the details of Black running away holding his arm. When Leo's house was shot up, a neighbor recognized Black hanging out the passenger window of a silver truck, shooting. Leo lived in Olivertown with His Godmom. She tried to get him and his brother out the hood after their parents died but as the saying goes, "You can take me out the hood, but you can't take the hood out of me."

Black was the only possible suspect in our minds. That's the only person who wanted Leo dead so bad. Leo wasn't a saint himself, he did dirt, but he was always very respectful to his elders. He had morals. He loved his family whole heartedly. He was a goofy person and a lady's man. He used his charm and sense of humor everywhere he went. I loved his personality. He was always so high in energy, friendly and outgoing. He could dance too. One of the best dancing guys in the neighborhood. He was a hood nicca at heart. Baggy jeans and big white tees. He always had a headband and wrist band on that matched his shoes. He had this nice thick gold chain around his neck and always had money in his pockets. He wasn't a bad child; he was just spoiled. He would get arrested for riding his Dirt bike around the neighborhood or for driving after his curfew time. Minor stuff that happened periodically, he was placed in juvenile detention centers several times which seemed to be the only way for a troubled young black male to be punished. Once released from the juvenile system, survival was the only thing to look forward to. So, he got into more trouble which came with more violence.

Leo and his older brother Tim had the same mom but different fathers. Leo's father married his mother when she was pregnant with him. He didn't really talk about his parents to me, but he often mentioned how he wanted to be in the grave next to them. I used to hear my mom and other adults talking about how their mom was crazy as hell and had a slick tongue, and she probably caused the car crash. No real facts were ever proven, just neighborhood gossip, therefore, out of respect I never asked Leo myself.

CHAPTER 6- MY SUPERHERO

"A true hero isn't measured by the size of his strength, but by the size of his heart."

-Zeus (God of the sky)

Everyone has a superhero, right? My Uncle was my superhero. He was more of a father to me than my actual dad. Him and my mom shared the same father. Uncle was the man that I knew I could run to. He gave me money, advice, and most importantly he listened to me. I was very open with my uncle, we got closer over the years. He didn't know how to roll blunts so I would roll them for him. He told me I made the best oodles and noodles and the best Kool-Aid, so he would pay me $5 when he was hungry to make them for him. I was always excited to cook for him. I even had an "oodles noodle Kool-Aid" song I used to rap to him as I prepared his very inexpensive meal. I would turn Jamaican and start flowing, "I'm a chef in the kitchen. Ramen noodle, beef or chicken? Grab the Kool aid, get to mixing. Ramen Noodles, beef or chicken?" I would repeat the hook in different accents and freestyle the verse. It was our little thing. A bond that could never be broken.

My uncle was my protection. His nickname in the hood was GOAT! He was "that nicca" in the hood, meaning he was respected, and I was that respected nicca's niece. He would ask me every day if anybody did or said anything foul to me and I would reply with the same answer "no uncle" even if someone did, I would still say "no uncle". I learned my lesson.

One night, I was sitting in Da Cut with my friends Veeta, Kim, and the twins when some dirty boy whom I didn't know was chasing people around with his homemade B B gun, it was made up of the top half of a huggee container, a red balloon around the rim and little rocks inside of the balloon that hurt like hell when you stretch the balloon back. We were scared, however we felt untouchable because we were the Cutt girls. Nevertheless, that dirty little boy didn't have a care in the world. He stood in front of us wearing a dingy 3x white tee, his everyday wearing dingy khaki Dickies with some off-white K-Swiss waiting for us to run, still we didn't budge. Vee warned him, "I wish you would little boy."

He started counting to ten, soon after, he noticed none of us move, he emptied his balloon clip contentedly. We all split up in different directions and I knew exactly where I was running to. "Uncle uncle uncle," I darted straight to Headquarters, busting through the door. My uncle was bagging up what seems to be crack cocaine, so I looked off to the side as I spoke. "Uncle some dirty little boy just shot us up with his BB guns."

"What? Who?"

"I don't know his name but he's ugly and got all these bumps on his face."

"Where he at?" He grabbed his gun, as we rushed outside and back to where me and my friends were sitting. I spotted Kim on an abandoned porch bent over, out of breath. I assumed she fell in the process of our escape from the enormous scrapes planted on both of her knees. She was bleeding and limping trying to get a good balance. Soon as she saw me and my uncle, she pointed in the little boy's direction. He was up in a tree laughing and climbing higher and higher.

I noticed him and told my uncle where he was at instantly.

"He's in the apple tree Uncle, right there" As we approached my uncle said calmly.

"Aye young nicca come down from there so I can holla at you man to man."

"Fuck you Old head, come get me" was dirty boy's response.

My uncle gave out a devilish laugh.

"You sure youngn? If I come up there it won't be pretty." My uncle warned.

"Come get me pussy homies!" he shot back.

My impatient Uncle removed his gun from his waist band and handed it to me. I was shocked that my uncle was about to climb up there. He realized the concern on my face then reassured me.

"Relax Niece I'm a handle him. He in my apple tree." My Uncle turned into Spider-Man, climbing the tree with no problem. He was much longer and stronger than any man I knew so my concerns went straight away.

Soon as he got to the dirty boy, branches and rotten apples started dropping. I backed up and leaned on the rail so I wouldn't get hit in the head by an apple patiently waiting for them to come down. My uncle had a tight gripped on the little dirty boy and he was crying out.

"Get off me pussy."

"Ouch that hurt."

"Let me go you going to break my arm."

"Ouch man I'm sorry!"

Once they were back on safe grounds, my uncle called me back over to the scene. I moved in command like the king calling his little princess over to the throne.

"Yes Uncle" with a quiver in my voice. Out of breath from climbing in and out of the tree he demanded "Shoot him where he shot you."

"Huh?" Completely thrown off.

I was standing there holding my uncles gun upside down.

"Hold the gun like I taught you and shoot this little nicca where he shot you." He wasn't playing with me this time, so I gripped the gun like he taught me.

"But uncle he only hit me in my thigh."

"Shoot this little bum as young nicca in his thigh then Niecy."

My uncle was drooling out of his mouth with smoke coming out of his ears.

The little boy wasn't laughing no more. He was quiet, crying silently. He knew he fucked up. A small crowd started gathering. I noticed Kim's mom holding Kim walking toward us yelling out something, but my surroundings started getting blurry. I was about to catch my first body was the thought going through my head. "Shoot him," I heard somebody chant out. "Do it!" I was frozen.

The universe started spinning backward as I was about to pull the trigger.

My uncle snatched the gun from me and put it in the little dudes' mouth. "Say Goodnight Little nicca." Everybody was tuned in. Eyes glued on what was about to take place.

By the grace of God, we heard Police sirens.

My uncle promptly let go of the little boy and tucked his gun behind his back.

"I'm a call you Lucky because you one lucky little mother fucker, next time you even think about looking at any of my little nieces I'm a kill you, you hear me?"

All the boy could do was shake his head. He appeared to be lost for words. I don't think he ever came so close to his death before this incident. When he got up off his knees, we noticed he peed on his self. Everybody knew the sound of police approaching, therefore, we acted normally and started walking away from what was about to be a murder scene. Ever since that day. Little dirty boy whom I learned later; real name was Andy never even looked my way again. He got teased for peeing on himself in them tan Dickies for years and I even started feeling bad for him, but I never said anything directly to him. Vee warned him, he should have listened. My mom heard about the incident from Kim's mom, and she reminded me to watch what I tell my uncle because she knew exactly how her brother was and if it wasn't life threatening, I'm best-off keeping things to myself. Rumor has it, my uncle had his own personal graveyard. From that day forward that's exactly what I did. Every time, on call, when my uncle asks if somebody gat a problem with me my response is "No Uncle."

CHAPTER 7- NUMB

"Our levels of gun violence are off the charts. There's no advanced, developed country on Earth that would put up with this"

-Barack Obama (First Black President of The United States)

"LEO GET UP. Please baby get up!"

"Wake up Leo. WAKE UP," I repeated to myself over and over again for hours.

The funeral home was cold, and it smelt like flowers. My face was burning from tears and my nose was tingling with snot. I couldn't take my hands off the side of the coffin and my eyes off Leo's lifeless body. He was only sixteen but, in his casket, he looked 21. He looked older, calmer, and mature. He looked like my husband at our wedding, and I stood by his casket like his bride. I wanted him to get up and kiss me so the Pastor could pronounce us husband and wife. After about 2 hours of crying, screaming, and sobbing, it was time to close the casket and move on with the funeral service.

When my friends grabbed me to turn me around so we could take our seats, I came back to my senses. The whole room was crying. Some was whispering, others were hugging each other. It was a moment I would never forget. We were defeated. Everyone looked and felt devastated. I took a seat next to my uncle and an older lady handed me some tissue along with a cup of water. Although I was dehydrated, I sat the water on the carpet, placing my face in my hands. So many people tried to console me, but of course I was numb. My vision was blurry. I felt so much pain in my heart that I started to feel nothing. My uncle was the only person who could get me to the car.

I don't even remember whose car I was in, I don't remember much else of the service, but I do remember as the doves were released and we all looked up watching them fly in circular motion, the clouds had a slight opening and sprinkles of raindrops splashed onto our beautiful faces. It was like magic, heaven's confirmation. At that very moment I cracked a smile. I felt relieved in a sense. "You made it baby," I mumbled through my smile.

When the cars from the cemetery pulled out, I stayed back. I wanted to talk to Leo one last time alone. He was in the dirt officially and from this day forward I had to go on without him physically. Emotionally empty was the best way to describe me. I said my last goodbye and right before I kneeled to throw a rose on the casket some more bullshit spiraled.

"Summer, let's go, we got to go. Homicide is everywhere up the hood." Lady Gee yelled out to me.

I ignored her because I was fed up with bad news. I let go of the rose and walked to the car.

FUCK!

AGAIN?

"Park right here Gee, we are going have to walk the rest, they got everything blocked off!" A relative of Lady Gee spoke.

"Damn, what happened?" She asked.

"Hell if I know, I'm with you," he responded.

We all jumped out with our eyes glued to the street.

I peeped Vee and April across the street. They seem to have a better view of the scene, so I motioned Lady Gee over.

"What happened y'all?" I asked.

"Girl they saying they found a body in a bandy." April answered. "We all are trying see who it is."

Vee gave me the look and it instantly gave me that gut feeling.

"Roll up Vee." I spoke with a guilty conscience.

"You got to blunt?" She asked.

"Fuck no, let's go get one," I instructed, throwing her hints to walk off with me.

"April hold this please, we will be back," Vee handed over her umbrella and Leo's obituary and we headed to the store.

Once out of sight I spoke out.

"Fuck Vee, I'm tired of this shit."

"Be cool bro. We don't know shit," she reassured me.

"What if they fingerprint the whole bandy doe?" I asked out of fear.

"Shut up Summer. They don't care to do all that. They don't give a fuck for real," Vee was getting frustrated.

"Bro you know I'm not going tell nobody," I said.

"Not even April bro, she can't hold water, or Lady Gee because you tell her everything." Vee stopped in her footsteps to make sure we were on the same page. I promised that I wouldn't speak a word. We grabbed the blunts and walked back to the scene. We knew homicide would take all day. Plus, the patty wagon wasn't even on the scene yet to take the body to the morgue. We rolled up and patiently waited for the body to come out.

"Yo Summer, let me talk to you right fast," I knew exactly who that was.

"Wzup DoDie?" I said irritated and restless.

"It's like that shorty? I just wanted to see if you were alright. You took Leo's death kind of hard," he spoke with concern, but I wasn't convinced. In my mind I'm like nicca you the reason we are standing right here right now, and I didn't even have a chance to change my funeral clothes.

"I'm going to be good; we lost a real one," I said.

"Homies that was my nicca, you know he told me about y'all," he shocked me.

"What? About what?" I couldn't believe what I was hearing.

"It's cool little mama I'm not going say nothing. I got your back. For my bro I'm going to protect you like he wanted to do." DoDie gave me a hug, but I didn't like the energy that went with it.

"Thanx Do, I appreciate it but I'm a big girl," I reassured him before I rejoined the crowd that was growing more and more.

"What the fuck he wants?" Lady Gee asked. From feeling the hole being drilled in my face from Vee, she was eager to know also.

"Nothing, he said he was just checking on me after Leo's funeral," I said.

Vee smacked her lips and rolled her eyes.

About two hours went by and the body was finally removed. Big boy Roy didn't have much family, his only brother was doing a sentence in federal prison and his crackhead Aunt just used him to get high for free. The hood was getting worse and worse. It was a kill or be killed neighborhood and I wanted out alive.

DoDie and the rest of the Darccide crew was on a rampage. DoDie especially, he had vengeance running through his veins. I feared him for sure. Me and probably everybody else in the hood. His background wasn't that sweet. His mom gave him up for adoption at birth. He was considered a crack baby. A lost child growing up in the hood surviving day by day. I knew to keep my distance from him because he was a force to be reckoned with.

CHAPTER 8- PROMOTION TO THE GAME

"No one wakes up one day and decides they want to become a drug dealer, or they want to be a stick-up kid. Those decisions are made after a series of events have happened in one's life."

-Michael K. Williams (American actor, Omar from The Wire)

June 16, 2005

It was my last day of middle school, graduation day and I didn't want to go. I was standing in front of my bed staring at my graduation outfit. My mom wanted me to dress a little girly, but my tomboy swag was off the chain. We agreed to do half girly half tomboy, so she bought me a tight blue jean outfit with a white lace halter top that had pearls on it with the all-white low-cut Air Force ones. I decided to finally wear my bling-out diamond name belt that Leo bought me. My hair was permed into a weave ponytail, and I had a nice bang and a princess diamond and pearled out hair piece. My jewelry was popping off crazy. I had a gold-plated necklace with my name SUMMER written on it, with the matching SUMMER earrings. My right hand consisted of 3 rings. My favorite ring had "SUMMER" in all capital letters on it, another with just the letter S, on my middle finger, and my pointer finger had a heart shaped diamond ring on it. I was in my Sunday's best sort of speak. I was HOT LIKE SUMMER. My bling out name belt was topping the whole outfit off. Everything was on point, but I still didn't care to go back to my middle school. Although I get to walk across the stage and receive my 8th grade certificate for my mom and family, I wasn't feeling it. I hated my principal for suspending only me and I wanted to burn the school down after Leo's death and my suspension.

When we went back to school for a meeting, the principal and my mom agreed to me staying home for the 2 months that was left of 8th grade because I was already top of my class and caught up on everything. They assigned ten different books to me and a ten-book report packet that I finished in less than 3 weeks. My extra time off school I picked up a bad habit of smoking weed. I smoked like a chimney. I was staying out later than usual. Life wasn't the same anymore. My old desires were long gone. I didn't know what high school my mom was signing me up to go to. She told me I wasn't going to the one where Leo was murdered, of course, I agreed with that decision. She was planning to send me across town, I was open for new adventures but nervous at the same time. I had to get my gear in tack for this new school. It was high school, so my gear had to be on one hundred and ten. Which only meant I needed more money.

Graduation was nice. I was feeling a little better seeing all my school friends again. Outside of the ones from St. Clair I barely seen anyone else. I missed my cool teachers too. They all wrote me letters after hearing about the tragic death of Leo. I cripped walked across stage with my jean jacket over my shoulder like a Don. I was bling out in all my pictures. The flash had my diamonds looking real, and then the all-white teeth with the all-white Air Force Ones was looking good. Karesha grabbed us a rental for graduation, and we all pitched in for a hotel to smoke and party. We were turning up for sure. Me, Vee, and April was all in the same grade, so it was our Special day. Although April went to a different middle school, she still partied with us. Kim, CC & Kayla was a grade under us. We were all the same age. I was the youngest of the crew by a few months but together we all were one.

The hotel party was off the chain. We invited some guys over. Kim and April knew some guys from April's other hood, and I ran into my older brother on my dad's side in the parking lot. He had some girl with him, and she was in the lobby paying for another stay. He lived on the east side of town, and he been telling me about some ecstasy pill he been selling for $10 a pill.

He said he had the hotel on smash. Making an average of $1,500 a night. I heard about ecstasy pills but wasn't into them like that. I was more interested in the money, so I told my bro to put me deep. Just by the way they were making people go crazy and all the nicca and bitches in the neighborhood was doing it I knew not to try it, but on the other note I also knew if I sold them business would be booming. Nobody was selling them in the hood. Everybody was driving to the East side of Pittsburgh to get them. I also heard rumors that when you popped an ecstasy pill, they would have you up for days, in my mind, I'm thinking why would people want to be up for days? But never mind that there was money to be made.

My brother told me to save up $600 and come see him. We exchanged phone numbers and departed. When I got back to the hood my mind was seriously working on where I was going get $600 from. I had about $27 to my name and I was stretching that for the long run, then it came to me. I remembered finding a baggy of crack wrapped up in some aluminum foil in an old jacket of Leo's that he had let me wear one cold summer night. I ran inside my room, searched for it, and then rushed out to present it to crackhead Seedy.

"Seedy check it out," I yelled.

"Wzup little Bo? It better be good because you are taking me out my nod," he limped over to me.

"I got to ask you a few questions" I motioned with my hand to show him what I had.

"Let me see" he reached for it.

"Naw old head, you aren't slick. How much you think I could get off this?" I asked.

"Shit give it to me, we split $100 for you $100 for me," he said licking his lips.

I knew I had to play his game to get what I wanted.

"Alright so what you are saying is, it's only worth $200?" I questioned.

"Yes, little girl, now give it to me so I can see if it's any good!" He shot back with his beady red eyes.

"Naw Seedy I know it's good, I was just wondering how much it was worth. Thanx doe" I said as I walked away. Seedy thought he was smooth, but I wasn't born yesterday.

As I finished my investigation, the only way I would know it's worth for sure was to take it to headquarters and weigh it on the scale. I learned a little bit of the game by observing when I was in headquarters. They always had crack on the table. Either they were weighing it, cooking it, or bagging it. So, I made my way to my uncles. I was a little hesitant, but I was eager to make some money.

As I approached the back door, Crackhead Kelly was standing out there.

"You can't go in young lady, your uncle busy," she informed me.

Crackhead Kelly was a nice crackhead. Yes, she did drugs, but she was sweet, she was my uncle's favorite. He told me they used to be best friends back in the day. So, if I couldn't talk to him, I knew I could talk to her about what I had in my pocket. I never questioned why I couldn't go in because I was street smart and besides, I was on a whole nother mission.

"Auntie Kelly how much can I make off this?" I showed her.

"What girl? Where you get that from?" She asked.

"I found it in one of Leo's jackets he gave me," I spoke with honesty.

"Hold up, stay right here I'm going to see if your uncle still needs me to guard the door. Put that away, I'll be right back," she dashed off thru the same door that she just said I wasn't allowed to enter.

30 seconds later she was back out the door with her pipe in her hand and some balled up dollar bills in the other.

"Let's go," she instructed me.

We headed to the city steps. At the bottoms of the steps, it was dark from the light pole being shot out, so we were safe right there.

"So, you think you dun growned up?"

"You want to sell this shit that will fuck your mind up huh?" She asked me catching off guard.

"Not really Auntie, I really want to sell ecstasy, but I need $600 to start. I rather sell pills than crack." I responded.

"Listen what you really want to do is stay in school and get ya education. You know I dropped out in the 5th grade. Watched my mom Overdose in front of my eyes off this here drug. Foster home after foster home until I ran away at 14 and started trading sex for money and a place to stay." She spoke with such pain.

"Damn Auntie foreal?" I was now concerned.

"Hell yea this crack rock is dangerous girl. I got hooked by an older guy I was sleeping with. It was the go-to drug that numbed my pain away when I was down and out. Promise me you would never try it and I'll help you get to your $600."

"I Promise Auntie, On Leo I would never smoke crack, Homies," I was sure and determined.

"Listen, I can't have you out here with this, so I need you to go to the bandy at the end of the court and wait for me. Your uncle and your mom would kill me. I will make the money for you, okay?" She asked and told me at the same time.

I trusted her so I did as I was told and waited.

1:00am came and went, 2:00am came and went and when I noticed the time, it was 3:05am and then I heard Auntie. I dosed off every now and again sitting in the bandy doorway. She had it nicely set up inside. An old couch and an old TV sitting on a crate. But I stayed by the door to wait on her.

When she came in, she had the biggest smile on her face. Aunty Kelly had about 4 teeth left, and they were all rotten, but she was just the grinning hard. She pulled out all this money that was balled up and we started separating the ones from the fives and the tens from the twenties. It just so happened to be check day, so business was good. That's what she assured me. I had no idea what that meant but from the look of things I was almost at my goal. We counted $685 altogether which was way more than Crackhead Seedy said I could make. I handed Auntie Kelly the $85 and she handed it back.

"Listen Baby, you my girl, I would never do you like that. I got my high on, you keep this. Now go on home and get some rest. And don't tell nobody what we did. If you find some more come find me!" I was feeling grateful and ran home thinking in my head how my mom was about to go hard on me for coming in so late, but to my surprise her car wasn't even outside, so I went in, got in the shower and went to bed. When I woke up, I felt good. I had $685 dollar off a little bag of crack and wanted to do it again and make more. My mom was snoring from her room. She probably came in super later than me so she would be asleep a little bit longer. I managed to get back out the doors before she woke up. Hitting the block with my new cash I felt like new money.

I dialed up my brother's number to reassure I was ready for him.

"Who this?" He answered.

"Your big sister punk I thought you saved my number?" I replied.

"Oh, Wzup sis, you mean my little sister, naw I never save numbers. You got to remember them in ya head, I got it now," he said in his laid-back tone. He was so calm and collected.

"I'm ready bro I got a$6-," he cut me off.

"Come see me sis, you know where I'm at, never discuss business over the phone," click!

I looked for Lady Gee so she could give me a ride. I knew she wouldn't tell me no.

Once in the car headed to the hotel where I once seen my brother. I gave Lady Gee the run down on how I was trying to sell ecstasy pills and how I made almost $700 the night before off a little bag of crack. She was so proud of me like I accomplished so much. It never dawned on me that what I was doing was wrong, plus I was so protected by so many people that encouraged me. They taught me new lessons along the way, and it was so easy. Easier than taking candy from a baby.

As I exited Lady Gee's vehicle she yelled "I'll be back in an hour. I got to do something for your uncle."

"Ok, I'll be ready," I said as I walked in the entrance of the hotel.

I heard her yell out again. "Be Careful."

I smiled as I reached the elevators.

Once on the 2nd floor I looked left and right to see what way my brother's room was. Room 233 was left so I headed left.

"Knock knock."

"It's open sis, I seen you pull up. Who that sexy ass bitch that just dropped you off? She should've come in with you,"

He said, rubbing his hands together. His girl smacked her lips and got up to go in the bathroom.

"Don't worry about it nicca I came to discuss business," we smiled at each other, hugged and got right to work.

An hour later I had the whole rundown about how to turn money into gold. He gave me the ingredients and lesson on how to move. Only 13, I was already adventuring the world, which was what it felt like.

He gave me 2 Jars of pills. Although I only had enough for one, he let me slide and said I owed him after I moved the whole package. See, pills were a lot different than crack. It was less mess and already ready to go. A jar consisted of 100 pills with different logos on them. My brother taught me to have flavor so the customer could have a variety to choose from. He gave me 50 yellow alligator, 100 blue dolphins, and 50 green Benjamin Franklin heads. "The blue dolphins are booming in the streets sis and you probably going sell out of them first, so before you run out holla at me. Never wait until last minute to flip ya bread!"

He walked me outside so he could greet Lady Gee when she pulled up. He opened my door when she arrived and they exchanged numbers with his charm, and me and her was on our way back to the hood. She was blushing and asking me why I never told her about my brother on my daddy side. I was in another zone. I couldn't wait to make this money. Get these schools clothes and do it again. Lady Gee had a few niccas already waiting on me when we got aback so I was already ahead of the game. It's funny because the same niccas that was selling crack to the crackheads was my best customers. They used to be up all day and night off them things and every time they would see me around the neighborhood they would ask "Where they at?" I was one to never disappoint so they were always on me. My brother's advice on how to re-up before I was about to run out was a genius idea. Soon as I made enough to grab more I would re-up. Lady Gee would take me to my brother's meeting spot about three times a week. Business was booming. The summer was epic. I began to notice all the money I was saving and all the pills I had. I was making a killing. My mom or my uncle didn't have a clue what I was doing and never questioned where I was getting extra money and nicer shoes from. Until one afternoon.......

I was brushing my teeth at the sink. My teeth were my pride and joy. I had nice pretty straight white teeth. I loved to smile because I always got compliments on my teeth. When I was younger, about two years old, my older cousin knocked my teeth out from pushing me while I was in a power wheel. We were going downhill with no brakes. We crashed into a parked car.

I went face first in the car door and my front teeth shattered in my mouth. My aunt who was babysitting me at the time didn't tell my mom until the next day and when my mom seen me, I had a black eyes and bruised face. She rushed me to the hospital where they had to surgically remove the teeth out of my gums. My teeth didn't grow back until I was in the 3rd grade. Just imagine having no front teeth for seven years straight, so when they grew back, I took pride in my new set.

I spent most of my bathroom time at the sink brushing my teeth. My phone was vibrating on my bed, but I ignored it because I knew it was a customer calling for more pills. My phone was booming. It rung so much I kept it on vibrate so my mom wouldn't catch on to my private business.

Well, the person who was ringing my phone was also at my door knocking but everybody in the hood knew not to knock on my door. That was law. So, when I heard my mom's reaction to the person at the door, I jumped down the whole flights of steps in my house and rushed to the door.

"Yoooooo," I said, puzzled at the guy.

I was on my tipping toes behind my mom waving him off, but he didn't give a fuck. Soon as he seen me, he was like "You got some more X?"

I played dumb "What X nicca? Get off my porch with that stupid stuff?"

"Oh, my bad Lady Gee said you be having all the flavors," he continued to spill all the beans.

"Lady Gee what?" My mom interrupted.

"Nothing mom, he is tripping," I said.

She slammed the door on the little boy, but she wasn't done with me.

"So, you selling ecstasy pills for Lady Gee? You a runner now? That's where all that money been coming from?" She was livid.

"No mom, he doesn't know what he's talking about," I said trying to walk away.

"Don't fucking walk away from me little girl, you're not fucking grown Summer, your only 13," She yelled.

"I know mom, and I'm not selling nothing for nobody." I ran upstairs to gather my pills and tuck my money so I could get back outside before she kills me. I was upset with myself because today for some reason, I took extra-long in the bathroom and had my phone ringing knowing how these nicca be about these damn pills.

As I was walking to the front door my mom wasn't finished. "I'm a go see about Lady Gee," she said.

"I don't care mom she is going tell you the same thing I'm telling you. I'm not selling pills for her. I swear, On Leo I'm not," was my last words as I left. I reassured myself that she wouldn't go ask Lady Gee because she had to believe me after swearing on Leo. She knew I would never lie on his grave.

When I approached the Cutt I seen my uncle spanking my little sister's mouth. She was crying hysterically and trying to run away from him. My uncle never put his hands on us so I knew she must have done something bad. "Where your damn mom Summer?" He yelled out at me. "She in the house," I said nervously looking at my little sister for answers. "I just caught ya little sister smoking cigarettes with her friends in the woods," he was furious.

Confused that my little sister did something bad I ran back in the house to tell my mom her brother was outside with her youngest daughter, and she did something worse than me.

My mom was smoking a cigarette when I ran back inside, and I already knew these chains of events was about to drive her insane.

My uncle took my sister inside and I made a run for it. Straight to Lady Gees so I could put her deep about my mom coming to ask her anything about me. When the coast was clear that night, I came back home to find my uncle still inside discussing my mother's two daughters with her. They looked like they were having a serious meeting, so I tried to go straight up the steps but of course they stopped me. "Get ya ass down here," my mom said with a little aggression in her voice.

"Fuck," I said silently in my head.

"So, my oldest daughter is selling ecstasy pills and my youngest daughter is smoking cigarettes already?" "Thirteen and eleven?" She said shaking her head. She had an ashtray full of cigarette butts which mean she smoke her whole pack in one day. I didn't say nothing because I was denying all accusations. She continued.

"Then the little bytch think she slick because I asked Lady Gee and of course she lied for her," She turned to me. "I know you told Lady Gee to lie for you. I'm not slow Summer. I did the same shit you're doing when I was your age." I still stood there silent. My uncle finally spoke up. "Man listen Sis, my ears are out in these streets, and I haven't heard a thing about her selling ecstasy pills, and I know for sure my niece isn't selling no pills without letting her uncle know first," he said as he winked at me. I was really nervous because I was scared of both of them, and I didn't know if they were asking me a question or telling me something, so I just stood there quiet.

"Look what you did to my daughter Goat."

"She ain't saying shit. Oh, you sticking to the street code now huh?" My mom asked as she got in my face.

"Chill Sis don't hit her," my uncle said taking up for me. "Why not, I just beat Micia's ass?" She barked back.

"Yea and that's enough. Micia shouldn't be smoking cigarettes at the age of 11 at least Summer isn't popping pills. She a hustler just like you and me," he said.

"You always taking up for her Goat," she said as she backed away.

"Honestly sis, we fucked up by raising these kids like this. Our dad did it with us now look at us. History repeats itself. We can't be mad at nobody but ourselves." They both agreed and my mom told me to get the hell out her face. I politely went in my room. I was exhausted. Soon as I dozed off my little sister knocked on my door.

"Come in" I said.

When I noticed it was her, she climbed on my bed. She was still shaking up from the whooping she got from my uncle and my mom. I felt bad for her because she got aa whooping and I didn't. But I told her myself she shouldn't be smoking cigarettes. I hated cigarettes and then we both dozed off in my bed. Me and my sister was only close when my mom was mad at the both of us. Any other time, my mom was usually on her side or mine and that's how we lived in a household full of girls. So, when our mom was mad at both of us which was rare, we stuck together. We had a different type of love. We came out the same coochie, so we had no choice but to stick together. I didn't want my little sister smoking cigarettes, weed, or any drug for that matter so I had to keep an eye on her and her friends a little closer. I was so caught up in my life I forgot I had to protect her, which I vowed to do from that day forward.

CHAPTER 9- SUMMER VACATION

"A vacation is what you take when you can no longer take what you've been taking"

—Earl Wilson (American journalist)

I thought I was going to be selling ecstasy pills and getting money all summer, but my mom had different plans for me and my little sister.

I heard her making plans for the 1st of the month which was July 1st. I don't really recall what the discussion was about, but I was interested. She was having conversations with her oldest brother on her mom side about driving to her oldest sister home in Maryland. The 1st was pay day and she said she would be ready early morning. So, all the end of June I seen her packing around the house. One night some girl and a gay guy knock on our door.

"Go get the door Summer, it's Ayonna," she instructed me. Ayonna was the neighborhood clothes booster. She was an expert at stealing clothes.

"Hi little Bo, you are getting big," she greeted me when I let her and her gay friend in.

"Hi," I said and sat back down on the couch.

"Hey Little ladies, Hey BO BO," the gay friend spoke.

"Aye Wzup Cousin," my mom said as she got up and hugged him. "Speak to your cousin Day Day"

"Hiii" me and my little sister sung out together in tune. We hated meeting new family members. It was annoying. Now we got a new cousin who is looking like a grown man but talking and switching like a girl.

"Uhn uhnnn Summer don't be rolling your eyes at me, you used to be my little baby. I used to have you geared up when you were like two months, ask your mom," he shouted.

"Yup, you sure did because, I remember them blue jeans jumpers you got her way before any babies was wearing them," my mom said cracking up.

"Yes hunny, when Ayonna told me she had an order for Bo I was like Who? My Cousin Bo? Oh, I'm coming, Bo used to be my #1 customer back in the day. And I see you still got your kids geared up. Go head Bo," he spoke with such pride. I started to like him, he had good energy in him, and his approach was bold, so eventually I loosened up.

"What y'all get me?" I finally spoke out.

That's all they needed to hear. Ayonna started pulling out big shit. She had jackets, shorts, scarfs, swimsuits, sandals, nail polish, underclothes, hats, all named brand, anything you could name she had. My mom handed her a wad of cash and they lingered for a little while then they left. On to the next paying customer.

When they left, my mom got on the phone and said she was now officially ready for the 1st.

Oh, she was but me and my little sister had no idea what our mom had up her sleeves.

The 1st came quick. I didn't get to re-up the night before like I planned. I got a text from his mom saying he went to jail. His mom said something about domestic violence between him and his girl. I only had about 20 pills left and didn't want to sell them until I had more.

When I woke up the morning of July 1st, my mom was playing music and throwing bags of stuff down the steps.

As I walked to the bathroom she turned around and told me to wake my sister up and get dressed. "Put something comfortable on, we riding to Maryland."

"Maryland?" I questioned "Mom I don't want to go to Aunt Dot's house," I whined.

"You don't have a choice, now wake your little sister up and get dressed before I pop you up upside your head." she spoke with such aggression.

After doing what I was told I was just moping around, so she told me to get out of her face until my Uncle Wyatt pulled up. I ran to Vee's house. I couldn't believe we was about to drive four hours to Maryland. My mom been tripping lately.

"Bro ain't no weed in Maryland," I said to Vee.

"You'll get over it when you get up there. Call me if ya cricket phone work all the way out there. My boost is global," she teased me about my cricket cell phone.

"Alright bro I will, I'm a miss you," I said as I reached out to her for a hug. "If my phone doesn't work, I'm a write you."

"Bitch bye you aren't going to jail," Vee said as she shoved my arms away from hugging her. "I will see you when you get back to the hood."

We both laughed as I walked back to my house. Vee was so fucking tough. Never the one to show emotions. I was going miss her for sure. I was pissed I had to leave the hood. So comfortable in my zone but also feeling a little grateful that I had family in other states. I walked past the grown-ups and straight to my room to stash the rest of the ecstasy pill I had left. I glanced around my room, said my goodbye to Little Bow wow and the rest of my wall poster and headed to the car.

The drive to Maryland was cool. I was high the first hour, so I slept the entire time. When I woke up, I seen a bunch of farms and farm animals. I shook my sister a few times so she could wake up and see the farm animals. She really wasn't pressed though. My uncle played his music the whole ride and my mom probably smoked about 10 or more cigarettes. I constantly checked my phone for service so I could message Vee, but it showed no service bars the whole ride.

It was getting hotter and hotter as we got closer and closer to my aunt's house in Maryland. We stopped once at McDonald's to use the bathroom and get something to eat. My uncle assured us that we were only 25 minutes away. My mom crossed the street to get more cigarettes and a few scratch-off at the gas station while me and my little sister ate our Chicken nuggets and French fries. I stayed woke the rest of the ride. I was curious about Maryland. We came one summer before, but we were much younger then.

"Welcome to Gaithersburg Maryland," is what the sign read as we entered my aunt's community. The community was so beautiful. It was so clean, and the air was refreshing.

"Fuck weed bro, homies I wish I had an aunt that lived out of town. When I grow up, I'm out of Pittsburgh." she spoke with high gratitude.

"Man, you don't understand, Maryland is boring, nothing going on up there. All these foreign people and Deer's everywhere. It's so quiet and there's nothing to do," I said.

"Bitch u tripping, pass the blunt so I could get high with you," Vee said.

I realized I was holding the blunt way too long and laughed out loud.

"Yea you right Vee I am tripping," I responded relighting the blunt and passing it to her.

We both burst out laughing and then began walking to the store. To get to the store from Vee's house we had to pass my house and I was hoping my uncle wasn't there yet.

Soon as we got close to my house, I seen my uncle's red Taurus with the tinted windows.

"Fuck, my uncle is here already," I smacked my lips.

My Aunt Dot was married with two children. She was the crazy Aunt out of all my grandma's daughters. She was the oldest and used to beat boys up when she was younger. She is very outspoken, and the family was so happy when she left Pittsburgh. She was the one that got a lot of shit started in the family. She was the "shit starter" that's what all the grown-ups would say. Moving to Maryland was the best decision she ever made. She gave her children a better future. Her son was the oldest of my grandma's grandchildren. He was 23 and enrolled in the Maryland Police Academy. He was the cousin that was pushing the power wheel when I lost my front teeth at the age of two. His name was Antwan and his younger sister's name was Lashay. Lashay had all the old Barbie and baby dolls that my little sister loved playing with. She was 18 and knew a lot about sex. I couldn't wait to tell her about my experience with Leo. The person that I was anxious to see was my Uncle Drew. That was my main man, he was a true comedian. That guy could make you laugh from sunup to sundown. He knew every funny movie you could name. He could change his voice to any comic alive. Uncle Drew was known for getting drunk, putting on one of my aunts' dresses, wig, red lipstick and performing the funniest show in the world.

They were all standing under their apple tree like a big happy family when we pulled in their driveway. My mom jumped out to hug her sister that she hasn't seen in a few years. We joined to hug our cousins. Our summer vacation began. My Aunt made plans for us all to go swimming on the first day there. She was a fish when it came to water, and she could swim very good. She told us that all the kids our age would be at the swimming pool and my other cousins on my Uncle Drew's side would be there too. I was excited to hear that because them are the only kids our age that we knew in Maryland. My Uncle Drew and his family are originally from the East side of Pittsburgh but they all one by one moved to Maryland to create a better life for their families. When my aunt and uncle left Pittsburgh, I was about five years old. I have a slight memory of them back then, but it's all told stories. My Uncle Drew had a great government job in Maryland. He was a bus driver and was making good money. They had a big, beautiful house and a nice big Expedition Truck. Their life was looking good in my eyes. I was thinking when I grow up, I wanted to leave Pittsburgh too so I could have a life like theirs.

Maryland was so much bigger than Pittsburgh. Growing up in little old St. Clair Village was like a needle in a haystack compared to Maryland. You had to drive to get to everything. Anywhere we went was a 30-minute drive minimum. There were no gun shots at night. No smell of marijuana in the air. The thing that I noticed the most was the sidewalks and streets were always clean. No trash in the yards, even on the highway there was no garbage in the woods. It was so much cleaner than Pittsburgh. Maryland was a breath of fresh air, especially for me. I needed fresh air. I was grateful to have an aunt that lived out of town. With all the madness going on back home, Maryland was the vibe for the summer.

My mom and Uncle in the red Taurus got back on the road immediately after our arrival. My little sister was sad to see my mom go but I was filled with joy.

"Make sure you take care of your little sister Summer!" My mom instructed; I was already on it. "I know mom, I am," was my reply as I hugged her and then ran in the backyard to the basement door. My cousin Lashay's room was in the basement. She had her own bathroom, living room, and bedroom down there. "You lucky to have your own floor in the house," I said to her. "Right little cousin, I be sneaking my boyfriend in and out on the weekend," she chuckled out. That's when our boy conversations started. I had so much to tell her.

My little sister was still into toys and baby doll. Baby dolls was never my thing. I was into sports and clothes. So, the majority of the day my little sister was in the toy room where we were staying for the summer. I didn't mind it though because it kept her occupied while I was in Cousin Lashay's room talking about grown up stuff.

My aunt must of knew what I was up to because she would scream down the basement door every so often to check on me. My mom probably put her deep, I assumed. My uncle worked twelve-hour shifts, so I never seen him leave but was always eager for him to come home. He was the life of the house. He had one day off a week and this upcoming weekend he promised he was going to take us to the pool with his niece and nephew. We were excited, after all Maryland was getting kind of boring to me. It was so peaceful. Nothing going on. We stayed inside or on the balcony. People didn't gather around much around the community. They all had their own land. You would see neighbors cutting their lawn or taking the recycling bin to the curb every now again but that was it. I was sure looking forward to going out to the swimming pool to see some people. I wasn't used to the Maryland lifestyle at all, but I had a whole summer of it, so I had to get accustomed one way or another.

It was finally Friday. My uncle's only day off. We woke up early. I made sure me, and my little sister ate some cereal then brushed our teeth. We had matching swimsuit, thanks to the boosters back home. I gathered our beach bag like my aunt instructed while she packed our lunch. My Aunt Dot was more excited than us to go swimming. She told us over and over how glad she was that we came to visit. I guess she was bored too in this boring city. She grew up in St. Clair too, so she knew what the hood environment was like. Finally in the truck ready to go, we click our seat belts and headed to the pool.

It was only about Noon, but the swimming pool was jammed pack. It was ninety-eight degrees and rising. Maryland heat was a lot hotter than that of Pittsburgh. My Uncle met his younger sister and her two children at the gate while we went inside the pool area to find a good table and chairs.

We set up all our belongings, claimed our own chairs by placing our beach towel on the back of them and headed for the pool. I was kind scared of water, so I stayed near the shallow, but my little sister was a dare devil. She dove in the deep, headfirst with my aunt following her.

"Micia be careful," I shouted from the ropes that divided the deep from the shallow, but she didn't hear me. She was too busy going under water holding her nose. I instantly smiled because I could tell she was having a great time since we arrived in Maryland. I heard my uncle's voice and noticed he only had my cousin Raha with him. "Hi cousin," she yelled from where we placed our belongings. I was excited so I immediately exited the water to greet her. "Cousin, I missed you," I said while reaching out for a hug. "Wait wait your soaking wet," she said as I got water all on her clothes. We both busted out laughing. "Where Micia?" She asked. "In the deep with Aunt Dot," I said examining the water. I pointed at them soon as I seen them come up for air. My little sister holding on to my aunts back splashing water with her feet.

"Where's Jaha?" I asked referring to her older brother. "Oh girl, he didn't want to get wet today, he is going bike riding with his friends. He was in the car, he told me to tell yal hi. My mom about to drop him off," she continued.

"Oh ok, dang you got a accent now," I noticed.

"Be quiet cousin," she chucked back.

"Where's your swimsuit?" I asked.

"Under my clothes," she showed me as she lifted her shirt.

"Come on den, let's go down the slide," I said with glee.

She removed her clothes, and we ran off to enjoy our day at the swimming pool. My cousin Raha was a little older than me by a few months, but we always clicked. We were both tomboys at heart. She had two older brothers and she was the youngest child.

We swam until closing time. Snacking and drying off from time to time, we didn't want to leave. I was having so much fun with my cousin Raha and my little sister had her swimming partner, my aunt Dot. My uncle basically chilled out and got sun burn because he forgot to put sun block on like my aunt instructed him too. When we got out the pool to finally dry off, I asked my uncle if Raha can stay a night and he agreed. We jumped up and down holding hands like toddlers.

The ride back to my aunt and Uncle's house was quiet. We were worn out, exhausted. We all fell asleep but the driver who was my uncle, he was enjoying his day off anyway, so he had more plans when we got in. He pulled the grill out on the balcony while we all got in the shower to wash the chlorine off. I picked out me and my little sister's pajamas as we prepared to eat and watch some scary movies for the night. Everything seemed to be going smoothly until my aunt got aa call that would shake our happiness up entirely.

"ANDREW" my aunt yelled from her room.

"ANDREW ANDREW, we got to go to the hospital RIGHT NOW," my aunt ran past the hallway bathroom that I was in, and I felt her energy, from experience, I automatically grew familiar with her urge. "Summer y'all stay here, we will be right back, Oh My God ANDREW LETS GO."

Raha came out of the guest room and looked at me with confusion. "Where are they going?"

"To the hospital, she said something is wrong with somebody," I replied.

Raha must have felt something jolt through her body because her knees collapsed. I rushed over to her while she balled up. She instantly started crying. Now I was really confused. I knew this feeling all too well, but I was in a different state, a different town where you didn't hear gunshots or fights outside so I was trying to figure out what could be wrong.

Raha finally spoke. "I bet my mom and dad was fighting again. She said one day she was going kill him"

"Don't say that" I spoke with sincerity in my heart. "Let's Pray."

I knew a little about prayer and I knew how powerful it was from experience, and at this very moment I was hurting for my cousin who didn't have a clue what was going on but knew it was bad. I kneeled down beside Raha and began. "Father God thank you for everything you have done for us, we love you God, we don't know what's going on, but our aunt and uncle just rushed to the hospital after getting a phone call and we are scared. Father God protect Raha's mom and dad, guide them in the right directions, in Jesus' name we pray, Amen. Raha looked up at me and I showed relief in her eyes. We didn't have a clue what was going on, but my prayer did something for her at that moment. We laid on the living room floor with a pile of comforters under us. We were still worn out from earlier, but I couldn't sleep because my mind was racing a million miles. In the wee hours of the night, I heard my aunt and uncle come in. We all must have dozed off watching a movie. My uncle picked Raha up and carried her to the car. I jumped out my sleep when I heard them.

"What happened?" I asked with blood shot eyes. "Get some rest, we got aa long day ahead of us," my aunt said but that wasn't enough for me. "Aunt Dot what's wrong? Is Raha's mom, ok?"

"She going to be ok, but Jaha was ran over and killed on his bike by a drunk driver."

She spoke out with such harsh words. My heart started pumping so fast. "What?" I stuttered. My eyes filled up with tears. My mind started going overboard. I couldn't believe what she just said. "Where he at? Is he going to make it? Who was the drunk driver?" I had a million questions to ask. I knew I couldn't go back to sleep. I went to the bathroom to pee, but every step was a struggle. Once in the bathroom I locked the door and remained inside until morning. I prayed and cried and asked God why? Why Leo? Why Jaha? Why so young? Why do we have to keep going through this pain?

Here I am all the way in Maryland, four hours away from the hood and still my people getting killed. This was a whole new type of murder though. Jaha was killed by vehicle. Leo died by the gun. But the pain remained the same. The ending was very similar. Tragic.

Jaha and I were very close. He was the cousin that I had a slight crush on, he was older than me, and we were cousin through marriage. Him and my boy cousins were close too. They played together when us girls gathered. I had to get in touch with my big cousin MJ. Him and Jaha was homies.

July 4, 2006

The days were dragging. It rained for the past three days. I haven't seen or spoken to Raha since the July 1st and the passing of her brother. Today was the candlelight memorial for him and I couldn't wait to see my cousin and give her a hug. I shed many tears for the family and also for me because I was going through something that I couldn't control. I was distant to my little sister and my family in my aunt's house. There was a basketball court in the neighborhood that I walked to early morning and stayed as long as I could. I just wanted to

133

be alone. I missed my friends back home already. I was aching in my heart from death after death and I was bored in this quiet town. I knew the Fourth of July back home in the hood was jumping. Firecracker all day and night. Big cookouts. Everybody outside dressed to impress. Big community love. I felt like I was missing out, but I knew I wasn't. I was happy to be away but bittersweet of the current situation of losing my cousin Jaha. It started to dawn on me that no matter where you go. Death is everywhere.

Walking back to my aunt's home from the basketball court I seen my big cousin MJ bouncing his basketball in the driveway. I blinked a few times to make sure it was him and then screamed his name out so loud with so much excitement. "MICHAEL JAMES."

He turned around and we ran to each other with open arms. Although I just seen him back in Pittsburgh, seeing him in Maryland was way different. I missed him like no other. MJ was my best friend slash cousin. We were 11 days apart meaning our mothers (who are blood sisters) were pregnant at the same time. Funny story the family always tell us that our mothers couldn't stand each other when they were pregnant but me and my cousin bond/relationship was the total opposite. He was the male me. The boy I always wanted to be. MJ was everything to me. He was my all-time favorite cousin hands down and I had lots of cousins, you got to remember my grandma had six children, including four girls.

"MJ I was just thinking about you oh my God," I enlightened him after we released each other.

"Foreal" he said so calm and nonchalant, with his beautiful smile. One thing about my cousin that I admired the most was his humbleness. I wanted to be like him so bad. His swag, his talent, everything. We grew up very competitive. Always wresting and playing sports. Me being a tomboy I fitted in just perfectly. I hung with him, and his guy friends and he dated all my female friends. We had big dreams always talking about our future. So eager to be grownups and do what we wanted to do.

"I'm so happy to see you cousin." I still was smiling ear to ear.

"You already know I had to get up here when I heard about Jaha," he responded changing the mood completely.

"Man, cousin I didn't even get to see him the whole time I been here," I said shaking my head. MJ put his arms over my shoulder and we both looked up to the sky. The wind started blowing gracefully, like it was talking to us. I felt something spiritual in that moment. I felt Jaha's presence. It gave me chills.

Breaking the silence MJ asked, "where them things at? I know you brought them with you." I giggled because already my cousin was trying turn up. "I wish. Shit I probably would be rolling right now, you know it been a week since I haven't even smoked," I replied.

MJ reaches down in his high-top Nike socks and pulled a baggie out. "Got blunt?" He jokingly said while waving the marijuana in the air. "Nope but there is a little gas station like a mile down. Let's walk," I said. "Who going sell a pack of blunt to us in this nice ass neighborhood?" He reminded me of where we were at. "Right duh! hold up, let me go ask Lashay to get one for us, did you see her yet?" I said running to the back of the house. "Yeah, come on she was on the back patio," he instructed.

Lashay didn't smoke, she was more of a drinker, but she was cool and walked to the gas station with us to purchase a blunt. She said she was only doing it for Jaha, and we were grateful. She also made me agree that I would do her laundry for her the next time she washes clothes. MJ was always the lucky one, that's why I always wanted to be a boy. They got away with so much more than us girls.

The walk back from the gas station I showed MJ a trail that led to the back of my aunt's house. There was a small creak there also. Lashay went back home and me and MJ stayed by the creak.

"When u find this low-key spot?" He asked as he cracked the blunt down.

"It was raining hard yesterday, and my umbrella flew out my hands and I started chasing it and this is where it flew to," I responded shrugging my shoulders. "What?" He asked laughing so loudly. "You chased a damn umbrella in the woods cousin?" I laughed with him after he repeated what I said. "Yeah, nigga you know I like adventures." We both burst out laughing as we smoked and reminisced about life. About an hour went by and it was time to head back to my aunts for food. We were high and had the munchies. We weren't going to Jaha memorial till it got dark outside, so I had time to relax and enjoy the air conditioning in the house. I was feeling a lot better knowing MJ was down Maryland with us now. I didn't know how long he was staying but I already had my mind made up that whenever he was going back to Pittsburgh, I was going with him.

After Jaha Memorial we all went back home to get ready to attend his funeral the next day. I was exhausted from all the tears I shed and all the people I hugged. As I was dozing off, MJ tapped me on the shoulder to wake me up. "Want to smoke?" He asked.

"Hell, yea nicca, but where at?" I asked like I was not just falling asleep ten seconds ago.

"Everybody is sleeping let's go on the balcony" He whispered.

So, we went outside, smoked, talked, and chilled. I got bit up by like five mosquitoes out there and we decided to call it a night. Me and MJ fell asleep on the couch and was woken up by the smell of breakfast. My uncle was in the kitchen cooking. Lately he been quiet since the death of his nephew and that wasn't like him. "Good morning Unc," I said.

"Hey Summer Wzup, you ready to eat?" He offered. "Not really, I just woke up," I answered.

Then the jokes began. "Well round here in 20th and Wexton we call this a little twinny twin twin Nigga." he started with the famous quote of the movie Friday. Then when he didn't get a good laugh out of me, he walked to the stairwell and shouted "Is the TV on? I said is the TV on? NOOOO!" He knew that would get me. One of my all-time favorites, the movie Crooklyn. I smiled and he knew he had me. My uncle knew every quote from every movie. He was a walking charade.

Walking towards me he had a tray of food for me dancing and singing "I never go back to Georgia, I never go back to Georgia. What are you talking about? I ain't no punta, I ain't no punta, I'm Connie, I keeps my panties cleans," I burst out laughing.

It was now my turn to follow up with my favorite part. "Hold ya horses, give me two licorice sticks, ten Bazookas, some lemon heads, some fireballs, and some Boston bake beans."

He was always the perfect person to make my day. On one of the saddest days for us, having to bury a family member he was trying to lighten me up. He must have sensed that I suspected something was wrong with him. I ate, got dressed, woke my little sister up and got her dressed too. We sat on the porch until my aunt and uncle was dressed and then headed to the funeral.

Maryland funerals were much different than Pittsburgh's. Well, everything about Maryland was different. For my cousin's "going to heaven party," that's what his mom nicknamed his funeral, he looked beautiful. It's sad because I didn't see him that often especially this summer. He looked much older as I expected, even though everything was different. The room gave me Leo's vibes. No matter what city and state a funeral is held at, they all smell the same—like death. There was a Mime at my cousin's funeral. She was very relaxing to watch. She demonstrated our sadness and his happiness and gave us a better reason to smile. I didn't cry that much. I think my eyes ran out of tears from all the tears I shed in the last few months. MJ was beside me the whole time. My little sister sat with my aunt and uncle while Raha sat with her mom and close relatives. After the funeral it was time to eat, I was starving. MJ motioned me to the back of the funeral to smoke of course. And it was right on time because I needed to get high. I was so grateful to have a cousin like MJ. I was always protecting the family but now that he was around, I was protected. He was my lord and savior, and he knew it too.

"Cousin you ok?" He asked.

"Of course, now that your here," I responded.

"I am not going nowhere," he reassured me.

"I hope I don't lose no more people, I can't take it, I can't even cry no more tears," I spoke as my voice cracked.

"Yeah, I feel you, I been stopped crying after my dad died," he said bringing up old memories.

I hit the blunt and thought about MJ's dad and how nice he was to us. We were only seven when he passed but I remember it like it was yesterday.

We were sitting on my Porch when we heard gunshots and seen everyone running to Cresswell St. We were too young to run and be nosey. The gunshots were fired around 3:30 in the afternoon but we didn't get the news till later that day when all the grownups came back from the scene. Me and MJ always was mature for our age, so we knew what was up. MJ didn't show any emotions at the time and my aunt was super concerned, so they made sure I stood by his side at all times which was a blessing for the both of us because we loved each other like brothers and sisters. I didn't attend MJ's father's funeral because I was too young but when MJ came back, he told me all about it. Over and over, he repeated "I'm the man of the house now." That's all the advice the older people gave him, and he sucked it up quickly. Stepping up by all means. He leaned more towards the streets as we got older and nicknamed himself Gunnz and always had one or two guns on him at all times. I thought my cousin was crazy but when shit got real, he always came out on top. He was the youngest lieutenant in charge up the hood. We never talked about death but one thing we would always say is "I'm a die with mines on me" & "burying me in a suit" it was like his favorite quotes. I tried to be down, but he wouldn't let me. Only thing I was allowed to do was hide the guns when shit got hot.

I hit the blunt and started laughing out loud.

"Nicca, remember they threw you in the pool with your coat on?" He knew where I was getting to.

"Hell, yeah and you had to jump in with me to help me pick up my guns and bullets that sunk to the bottom."

I passed MJ the blunt.

"Everybody ran when they realized they fucked up," he took a puff.

"That's when I knew your name was really Gunnz. I was pissed I had to get in that cold as water to pick up them bullets." We laughed together.

"That's why I love you cousin, you always got me." He hugged me tight.

"I am going home when you leave Maryland." I completely changed the subject.

"Why? ain't nothing in the hood." He reminded me.

"I know but damn everywhere I go there's death. I could've stayed in the hood for all this." I said walking back toward the front of the funeral.

"Yeah but at least it's more peaceful here," he whispered because the grownups were staring. "I'm leaving when you leave." I repeated myself and meant it the second time around.

He didn't respond. We said our last goodbye to Jaha, stopped at the scene where he was hit, put flowers there and headed back to my aunt and Uncle's spot. Everybody was drained. We changed out of our funeral clothes and got into something more comfortable. I went to sleep immediately and woke up the next day to MJ packing up his suitcase.

"You leaving?" I asked as I stretched.

"Yea uncle D just got here," he answered.

"I'm coming." I jumped up and started looking for all my belongings.

"Chill cousin your better off here then St. Clair," he warned.

He had a point. I looked over at my little sister still asleep and decided to stay. I probably didn't have no other choice, but the truth of the matter was that I was on vacation and was so worried about home.

"Put your slippers on so we could smoke one last time before I leave." MJ told me.

We went down to the creek and smoked and laughed. Throwing rocks in the water watching them skip across. My uncle beeped his loud horn and that was the signal to head back up to the house so MJ can get on the road. I was not ready to be by myself again and my phone still wasn't working but I had to suck it up.

MJ left and I was back to being distant. I felt like I was in jail now and couldn't leave until the summer was over, so I made the best of it, taking it one day at a time. Raha didn't come over much because her mom wanted her closer to her. Lashay got a boyfriend and started being sassy towards me. My uncle picked up more hours at work to keep his mind busy. In the house the whole summer was me, my aunt, and little sister. They did girly stuff like polish their toes and play in makeup. That wasn't my thing. I stayed occupied by watching movies and going outside to the park to play basketball. The basketball court was a relief. It was therapeutic hearing the sound of the ball going swish thru the net. I was a three-pointer shooter and was getting better and better at my shot, making 7/10 every time. I was a defense player when it came to basketball so when I got the ball, I learned to shoot threes and get right back to defense. Running to the hoop for layups was too much energy. Besides, in my mind I did less work and got more points—win-win situation. Playing basketball everyday made me think about joining the high school basketball team when summer was over. I played more in middle, but I eventually quit because we never won a game. They never gave me the ball but always wanted me to play defense. I didn't like that, so I quit like four games in. But now that I was older and going to a new school, I was more interested. My new school was called Perry

Traditional Academy. It was located on the Northside of Pittsburgh and rumor has it that they were top five pick when it came to basketball for the boys' and girls' team. I was super interested and considered the rest of my summer vacation as tryouts, which helped my days go faster too.

Chapter 10 – ENOUGH IS ENOUGH

"Turn your wombs into wisdom"

-Oprah Winfrey (Billionaire media executive/Philanthropist)

Finally, summer was over, and school was a week away. Halfway back to Pittsburgh my phone started working again and I had a thousand text messages from all my friends and customers. From the alerts coming through my phone, I was highly missed. It gave me a great feeling inside as I headed home. I stayed up and read every message sent. I wasn't surprised at all the messages I received. People was texting me about ecstasy pills, wondering where I was at. I didn't tell nobody but Vee, but I knew my presence was missed. I learned that Reebok went to jail for selling weed and then a couple days later his twin brother Red was robbed and killed. Soon as we entered the hood, my senses came back. The smell was familiar, the air was familiar. The grass and row houses were beautiful to me. I missed my hood. I didn't know what I was going do first when we pulled up to my court. We got in town in the middle of the night, but I was so anxious that I couldn't sleep. When morning came, I burst out the doors to hit the cut and see the familiar faces I haven't seen in two long months.

First thing I did was walk to the candy store. I was tweaking my favorite snacks that only the hood stores sold. I got two of everything. The candy straws were like gold on my tongue as I devoured them.

As I was sitting on the city steps, I felt the hairs on the back of my neck stand up. Approaching from behind I heard a familiar voice. The last voice I wanted to hear on my first day back.

"Oh, you really Whoopi Goldberg now, you got all black and shit."

When I turned my attention to who was speaking to me it was DoDie. I swallowed hard.

"Hi Do," I greeted him.

"Wzup chocolate, give me a hug," he reached his arms out.

"You got taller and darker."

He was looking me up and down licking his lips. I smiled trying to play him off. But his hug was tight and extra.

"How was your trip?" He asked.

"It was Kool, I didn't do much but hoop," I responded shrugging my shoulders.

"Oh, you nice in hooping?" He asked.

"Yeah, I'm nice, I'm thinking about trying out for the team at my new school."

"Listen if you ever need some lesson come find me. I was the star player on my team back in the 90s, until I got hit up." He lifted his shirt up showing his stomach that looked to be split in two separate parts.

"Damn Do, what happened?" I was now concerned.

"Long story young lady let's just say I had to learn how to walk again, and talk again, but I am not complaining because it made me who I am today. One thing for sure and two things for certain is I would be in the league by now."

I never seen him look so weak and vulnerable.

"You Kool?" I asked.

"Fuck yeah young, I'm tripping, I just had a moment," he said and then walk away to meet a snap that was signaling him over towards them.

I tried to ease my way back towards my crib before Do recognize but he called my name out and caught back up to me. Something about his energy made me uncomfortable, then it hit me, but I was too late.

"FREEZE."

"GET THE FUCK DOWN."

"GET DOWN NOW."

I never thought in a million years so many cops would be surrounding me with guns drawn. "WHERE's THE DOPE?"

They asked over and over while shoving me and DoDie to the ground.

Immediately searching us.

"I don't have nothing on me, what are you doing?" I asked squirming on the ground.

DoDie remained silent. He didn't say a word or show no emotions. I felt something drip out my nose and started yelling

"Get off me, my nose is bleeding."

My nose must've started bleeding from my body overheating and all the shock that was running through my body.

"Let her up," one of the dirty cops instructed.

The cop yanked me by tank top and dragged me toward the rail. I tilted my head back to stop the bleeding.

"Relax Duggins, she looks like a juvenile."

The same dirty cop walked up on me.

"What's your name young lady, I'm Officer Wood?"

"I didn't even do nothing" I spoke.

"Sounds a little guilty to me, I asked you for your name," he replied this time getting in my face.

"He's Clean" another cops shouted out referring to DoDie.

They pulled him up from the ground and stood him next to me.

"Who's your supplier?" Officer Wood asked both of us.

"Your Mother," DoDie responded.

Officer Wood threw a punch at him landing right in the middle of his face. DoDie never showed any emotions, he sucked on the bottom of his lip and spit saliva mix with blood onto the ground where we were just face down on.

"Next time I see you make another drug transaction that's your ass Clinton, you hear me? I'm watching you. Have a nice day lady," and just like that they just walked away.

I was completely irritated; I went home to wash the blood off my face and ran back outside before my mom woke up. I didn't bother telling her about the cops because I didn't do anything and there was no need to give her a reason to snap out. I didn't want to hear her mouth. I walked to the basketball court to see if anybody was there, but it was still too early, so I sat down and started eating my snacks on the bench under the tree.

"Fuck wrong with you?" Vee scared the hell out of me, catching me off guard.

"Girl I was trying get away from Dodie's ass, he makes my fucking skin crawl." I said with a shiver.

"Let me find out you brand new now, got that Maryland blood in you all of a sudden," she shoved me.

"Naw I'm good now, shit first day back that's the last nicca I wanted to see," I reminded her. "Then soon as I tried to dip off this nicca run towards me and the fucking cops jumped out on us."

"For what?" She asked.

"His hot ass was bussing a snap" I responded.

"They probably on him about Red." She was about to put me deep but then we had company.

"Summeraaaa, Wzup baby" Lady Gee greeted me with open arms.

"Wzup old head I missed you," I said as we hugged each other.

"Yea yea yea these streets missed you, when are you getting right?" She asked referring to the ecstasy pills.

"Shit it look like the Block is hot, but I'm going hit my bro up right now, let him know I'm back," I said whipping my cricket phone out.

Just that fast and easy I made one call and was back on. The rest of the summer was all about getting money. Even though the block was hot from all the killings and drug dealing, they weren't worried about me. They had bigger fish to fry.

School was starting soon. I had a pair of dickies pants in every color. I bought a lot of football and basketball jerseys. Wearing them reminded me of Leo. I had three pairs of Timberlands.

The butters, all black, and the blue jean ones. My mom got me all my underclothes, twenty outfits, a mink coat for the winter and all my school supplies. My high school year was looking bright, and I was ready.

I entered high school like a boss, standing out like a sore thumb. First day of school, I wore my favorite football team jersey, 89 Hines Ward from the Pittsburgh Steelers. I had the all-black home jersey on with some all-white dickie pants and some black Timberlands. Kinky Twist in my hair and all my gold jewelry on with my diamond name belt. My swag was different and going to a school on the other side of town was really different but surprisingly they embraced my uniqueness, and I became a people magnet. Everyone was curious of who I was and what hood I was from. I made school friends almost immediately. They liked my charm and my sense of humor. I told everybody I was from the South Side, St. Clair Village to be exact. They heard of the neighborhood from the news, and they see the hood qualities in me. I was hood in every way, and I was a female, they loved that. Of course, I had haters, but I never got into a fight at school, and I kept Straight A's throughout every high school year. I was very smart but was a class clown, always had a great personality and I was bold. One day towards the end of my freshman year, it was 101 degrees in school, and I decided to pull the fire alarm. During fire drill the principal said she was checking the cameras for any foul play, and I left school, me and a few other school friends. We laughed so hard and mocked our school principal the whole day. One of my friends was a senior and had a car so we jumped in with her and she took us to her hood. We vibe out, smoked some weed and chilled with her hood niccas.

There was this one guy who stood out the most to me. He was on a dirt bike and had mud all over him. I wanted him and knew I was going get him. See the guys in school was cool but all the good ones had girlfriends. This one was rough looking, dark chocolate, nappy braids, with nice teeth. I walked over to him saying, "Let me ride!"

"You can't fuck with this big boy," he responded with the sexiest raspiest voice I ever heard.

"Well, ride me then," I said telling him more than asking at this point.

I climbed on and he started it up. I wrapped my arms tightly around him and inhaled the sweaty fumes coming from his sweaty body. He turned around and said,

"Hold on, ain't no brakes."

He jerked off in mid-air causing us to do a wheelie and raced off in the project. I was so terrified but was so turned on at the same time. My vagina was so moist, I tried keep my composure by closing my eyes tight and clutching my legs against his. He gave me such a rush.

I was completely turned on; he began to slow down. I opened my eyes and soon noticed why he slowed down.

"I want you to jump off and run," he yelled out.

The police were approaching us, and he was about to make a run for it. I knew this all too familiar from witnessing Leo being harassed over and over again by the cops. They hated dirt bikes in the projects. I gained my composure and jumped off on que, running in the Opposite direction. I ran back to where my school friends were. Out of breath and laughing at the same time at what an amazing day I was having. I had such a rush in my veins. I was high off life and weed. We watched the guy get away from the police and then we left because the project got flooded with cops. I had that guy on my mind the whole rest of my day. I had to find out who he was. I had to have him. It was something about him. I felt that feeling I used to feel with Leo. The next day in school I was going to do some research.

Well at least that's what I thought. When I got to school everybody was looking at me. The teachers were side eyeing me and the security was whispering to each other when I walk thru the metal detectors. About 4th period the principal came over the intercom.

"Can Summer Hudson Report to the principal's office? Summer Hudson. Thank You."

My classmates started pointing and making loud noises. My teacher sent me out the class. I knew I was in trouble but remained calm. I thought I was hidden from the cameras when I pulled the alarm. The girls that I left school with all stood around me when it happened so when I got to the principal office, she couldn't tell me nothing.

Walks in*

"Have a seat," principal Bissel demanded.

She was pissed. The energy in her office was tensed.

I didn't say a word as I took my seat across from her desk.

"Summer, your one of our top students in the freshman class. I know you had a hard year last year and was looking for a positive shift at this new school. All your teachers speak highly of you and your grades are awesome."

I stayed quiet but was confused about if she was about to reward me or kick me out of school.

"We spoke with your mother; she will be arriving shortly to join us."

At that moment I had to say something.

"For what?"

Then the door opened. In came my mom along with the security guard Mr. Mike.

"Greetings Mrs. Hudson," my principal greeted my mom.

"It's Ms. Hill," my mom corrected her. She was already fuming.

"My apologies Ms. hill, sorry we had to drag you all the way across town to meet with us, but we had a false alarm yesterday during school time and your child Summer was one of the names that was given to us."

"For what?" I asked again.

"Quiet Summer, let me explain," Mrs. Bissell said.

"The fire alarm went off around 12:15 pm yesterday afternoon and there was no sign of fire. A student came forward after we checked the cameras and seen a group of girls gathered near stairwell three."

"We spoke with every girl this morning and they all admitted it was Summer who pulled the fire alarm."

"What?" I blurted out standing to my feet.

"Have a seat," security guard Mr. Mike told me.

"Man, I didn't do nothing, show me the cameras," I said in my defense.

My mom wasn't saying anything but that meant I didn't know how she was feeling.

"Y'all can't just blame me, I don't care what nobody said, show me the camera of me pulling the fire alarm." I was serious.

I knew I was fully covered when I pulled the alarm, so I wanted them to show me. A part of me just wanted to see the camera just to make sure I was covered. I picked two tall girls to come with me just so the cameras couldn't see me. I planned to not get caught, so the fact that the girls already snitched was blowing me. I'm from the projects, we never snitch. I was furious that I was being told on.

The principal rose up and left out with the security guard. Finally, when me and my mom was alone, she turned to me and asked.

"Did you do it Summer? Just tell me!"

"No mom, swear they don't have me on camera pulling the fire alarm."

I looked around the office for any voice recorders or cameras.

"Tell them to show us the camera."

She reassured me before the principal rejoined us. "Oh I am."

Door opens* in comes Mrs. Bissell.

"Ok so we can't really identify Ms. Hudson actually pulling the alarm but we see her and a group of girls leaving the lady's room and walking toward the stairwell. We have everyone's statement saying she was the perpetrator. So were going to have to suspend you for ten days and charges might be brought upon you. If you admit your wrongdoing right now, I can assure you that no charges will be filed, and you can return to school in three days instead of ten. Last chance Ms. Hudson, we know it was you," Mr. Mike churned in.

My mom stood up gripping me with her and said, "Prove it Mrs. Bissell!"

"Ok will do, the principal stood with us. We will be keeping in touch. Have a great rest of your day, sorry to bring you so far from home Ms. Hill." Ms. Bissel reached her hand out for a shake goodbye, but my mom dismissed it.

We left out of the office and my mom still had me gripped up. The bell rung soon as we stepped out and students was gathering around the principal office as my mom pulled me out the school. Once in the car. She lit a cigarette, and the rest of the ride home was silent.

I was spoiled for real and knew I wasn't going be in trouble, but I grew concerned about the stress I been causing my mom. I was getting sick of it. I was madder at my principal for making my mom come to school than my actually guilty actions.

When we got home there was a ton of cops' cars out front of our court. We jumped out to see what the hell just happened. The neighbor signaled us over and informed us.

"Girl y'all just missed it. Crackhead Seedy got beat half to death. He was stealing from Headquarters," she told us.

"Is he dead?" My mom asked.

"Girl, damnear."

"Who did it?" I blurted out because my uncle ran Headquarters. That's all I was worried about.

"True whooped his ass," she said.

A sign of relief came over me. At least it wasn't my uncle Goat. True was one of the top dogs in the hood though, so Seedy had to do something serious.

I walked off from the gossip and went to the cut to get a better view. It was blood everywhere. The Cutt was taped off with cops everywhere. It looked like a murder scene.

"Why aren't you in school neicey?" My uncle asked soon as he seen me being nebby.

"They suspended me for something I didn't even do," I responded. Sticking to my innocence.

"Oh, ok well as long as you didn't do it, it doesn't matter," he said as he hugged me.

That's why I loved him. I knew he knew I was lying but still he never judged me. I could've told him the truth, but he knew the truth.

"Where your mom?" He asked.

"Over there," I directed him with my fingers.

He walked off to join her on the neighbors' porch.

I went in the opposite direction to find Lady Gee. She wasn't home and wasn't at the crime scene. She must be laid up with some new guy. Lady Gee was a very social woman. All the guys loved her. I seen Tim sitting on the city steps and decided to join him. "Wzup Bro?" I greeted him.

He was happy to see me.

"Sis what you are doing out of school?" He asked.

I rolled my eyes because everybody was about to ask me the same question for the rest of the day.

"I'm suspended for something I didn't do."

"So, what they say you did?" He asked as he rolled his blunt.

"They try say that I pulled the fire alarm but when they watched the cameras, they couldn't prove it and still decided to suspend me because some girls said I did it." I said without taking a breath.

"Damn sis you sound guilty as fuck," and we both burst out laughing.

"Man, Nicca I was hot as fuck in school, so I had to do something to get out of there." I finally admitted it.

He was running in circles cracking up. It wasn't that funny, but I needed the laugh too.

"You bad as hell sis Homies. What you say it was hot as hell, I had to go," he continued laughing. He had tears in his eyes as he tried to light his blunt up.

"Let me hit that brother," I reached out to take the blunt.

He passed it and blurted out.

"Sis I got another shorty pregnant, what I'm I supposed to do?"

"Do Resha know?" I asked referring to his girlfriend/baby mom.

"Hell No and don't you say nothing to her about it." He warned me as I passed the blunt back.

"So just tell the girl to get an abortion then," I told him shrugging my shoulder.

"She was until she found out it was twins."

He just put his head down.

"Woah my nicca, you in trouble, Homies."

"Tell me about it, Resha going leave me sis, I just know it."

"Damn bro, well congratulations and good luck because you are going need it."

He busted out laughing again.

"You funny as hell yoooo."

We both laughed it off and finished the blunt.

"Seriously doe, let me borrow a X I got you tomorrow," Tim asked with a slick grin. That nicca knew I didn't do credit, but he was different. Plus, he was Leo's big bro.

"Here man, you are going need this motherfucker and many more, I'm a be looking for you tomorrow too," I said as I dug in my left sock.

"You know I'm good for it sis, I just don't want to go in the crib and face her right now."

"Yea yea yea bro," I said as I headed to the candy store for some snacks. I didn't eat lunch in school because they suspended me right before lunch time and I had the munchies from that blunt.

As I made my way down the Cutt to the store something came over. My palms starting sweating and my left eye switched.

"What a day! And just like that. Another episode of crazy in the hood. It's always some shit going on, it can't get no worse than this." I was walking and talking to myself.

My phone vibrated in my pocket. It appeared to be a text.

It read: *M.J. JUST GOT SHOT HE AINT BREATHING*

I stopped in place and started praying out loud.

"God please get me out of this ghetto and show me the way, I know there's so much more to life, Amen."